Where the River Begins

Patricia M. St. John

MOODY PRESS

CHICAGO

© 1980 by
The Moody Bible Institute
of Chicago

All Scripture quotations are from the
New American Standard Bible.

Library of Congress Cataloging in Publication Data

St. John, Patricia Mary, 1920-
   Where the river begins.

   SUMMARY: A confused and misguided youngster stays
with a Christian family while his mother is institutionalized.
They help him discover the source of the nearby river and
the source of Christian life.

   [1. Christian life—Fiction.   2. Family problems—Fiction.
3. Foster home care—Fiction]   I. Title.

PZ7.S143Wh   [Fic]   80-12304

ISBN 0-8024-8124-8

13 15 17 19 20 18 16 14

Printed in the United States of America

Contents

CHAPTER		PAGE
1.	The Cherry Tree	5
2.	The River	11
3.	The Farm	17
4.	The Cherry Tree Again	25
5.	The Gang	33
6.	The Fire	43
7.	In Trouble	51
8.	Flight	59
9.	Refuge	69
10.	Questions	75
11.	The Source	83
12.	The Tulip Bed	95
13.	The River of Life	103
14.	The Swan	113
15.	The Homecoming	119

1

The Cherry Tree

"Francis!" shouted his stepfather, *"will* you behave yourself! Leave your little sister alone! It's crazy, a boy your size!"

Francis gulped down his mouthful and started the usual argument.

"I tell you, Dad, she kicked me first—she always does, and you always think—"

"I didn't."

"You did."

"I didn't."

"Francis, hold your tongue! Can't you see how you're upsetting your mother and bringing on her headache? Don't you *care*?"

"Well, I'm only telling you—"

"You just stop telling us then. Take your lunch and finish it in your bedroom and stay there till I call you. I'm dead sick of all this quarreling. Anyone would think you were a baby!"

Francis seized his plate, snatched a jam tart from the middle of the table, set it down in the middle of his gravy, aimed a last deadly kick at Wendy's shins, and made for the door. Her yells followed him down the hall. But he did not go up to his bedroom. He sneaked through the living room, stuffed his Star War

comic down his jersey, and streaked out of the back
door into the yard. He must not walk in front of the
kitchen window, where they were finishing lunch, so
he tiptoed round the house and made a run for the
hedge. Stooping low, he crept through the long grass
behind the apple trees and reached the cherry tree at
the very end of the yard in safety.

Nobody quite knew who the cherry tree belonged to,
for its roots were half in Francis's yard and half in
old Mrs. Glengarry's next door. That imparted an
exciting trespassing sort of feeling to begin with. It
was fun to peer over into other dangerous territory
and pretend he must not be seen, although Mrs. Glengarry had long ago noticed the dangling legs; and
when Francis's sandal had once dropped into her
lavender bushes, she had come out and handed it
back. She rather liked the dangling legs; they reminded her of something she had lost many years
ago.

But nobody from his own house had yet discovered
Francis's hiding place in the cherry tree, for it was
hidden by an evergreen and was not easy to climb. In
fact, climbing was impossible with a plate, so he finished his dinner crouched in the bushes, squashed his
tart into his pocket and jumped for the lowest bough.
He kicked up his legs to catch hold of it and hauled
himself up and over. Then, hand over hand, he
climbed to a big fork in the trunk where there was a
kind of seat and a hollow large enough to contain a
tin box.

Francis settled himself comfortably and checked
the contents of the tin box. It was all there—three
dinky cars, fifty football cards, and a bag of mints.

He ate up the crumbs of his tart and started to think over his position.

He did not mind being sent away from the table. In fact, when Dad was in a temper and Mum had a headache and Wendy was in a bad mood, it was far pleasanter to have lunch in the cherry tree. Nevertheless his heart was sore. Wendy *had* kicked first— she always did—and Dad always blamed him because he was the oldest, and it was not fair. If he had been Dad's son, Dad would have liked him as much as Wendy and Debby, and it was not true that he did not care about Mum's headaches. He did care, and he would do anything for his mother, but somehow he never got a chance to tell her so. *And Dad said I was naughty, and Mum always believed him, and it wasn't fair— Wendy kicked first, and they never said Wendy was naughty. Dad always blames me.*

His thoughts were going round and round in the same old circle, back to the same place. *It wasn't fair—it wasn't fair.* He said it to himself in bed at night, so that he sometimes would not sleep, and he said it himself in class so he could not listen to what the teacher was saying, and she had said on his last report that he was inattentive. Then Dad had been cross and said he was naughty again, and Mum had believed him. *And it wasn't fair.*

But here in the cherry tree it was easier than anywhere else to forget that it was not fair, because there were so many things to look at. He could see Mrs. Glengarry coming out, wrapped in shawls, to feed her cats, and Mrs. Rose, two doors away, hanging out her dish towels. He could spy on everyone's back yard and on beyond the yards to where cars and trucks

roared along the main street and on to where the
woods began and little hills rose behind with warm
acres of pink Warwickshire soil, farms, and pastures,
and somewhere, between two dips in the hills, the
river. It was March and the end of a wet winter. The
river would be flooding its banks in parts and nearly
reaching the bridges.

Then he looked round on his own yard. The cro-
cuses were ragged and dying, but the daffodil spears
were pushing through the grass. It was very quiet except for the birds, and he wondered what they were
all doing. Mum would have gone to bed with her
headache, and Dad would be with Wendy and Debby
because it was Saturday afternoon. He would probably take them to ride their bicycles in the park and
buy them ice cream. And, no doubt, he would soon
go up to Francis's bedroom to tell him that if he would
behave and say sorry to his little sister he could come
too. Francis had to admit that Dad quite often tried
to be kind.

But he did not want anyone's kindness, and he was
not going to say sorry to Wendy or ride his bicycle
with little girls, and he had enough money in his
pocket to buy himself ice cream. Spring was in the
air, and he would go off by himself and have an adventure. He would go to the river, and Mum would
not worry because she would be asleep, and Dad
would probably be only too glad to get rid of him.
He pocketed the mints and scrambled cautiously
down the tree, peering through the evergreen to make
sure the coast was clear. His bicycle was in the toolshed and not hard to get at. Another few moments
and he was out the gate pedaling madly and breathing hard. He had made it!

Francis had a vague idea of getting to the river, but he had never been so far by himself, and by the time he had reached the bottom of his road, he was beginning to wonder whether an adventure by himself would be much fun. He even found himself thinking longingly of Dad, Wendy, and the park and half hoped the others would catch up.

But they were nowhere in sight, and he suddenly realized that he was standing at the bottom of a street where the houses were smaller than those on his road and that down this street lived Ram, a boy from India who went to his school. He had never taken much notice of Ram. Nobody did, because he was very shy and small for his age, and he could not speak much English. But Ram had a bicycle and would be someone to share an adventure with. Francis pedaled to number 8 and knocked on the door.

Ram's mother came to the door, wearing a deep blue sari, her hair hanging in a braid down her back, and a tiny girl on her hip. She did not know much English either and looked rather frightened. She called Ram, who came running out and introduced everybody. His little sister was called Tara, and she stared solemnly at Francis with huge, unwinking black eyes. Francis decided that he liked her much better than Debby.

Ram's mother seemed pleased that Francis had come to invite Ram to go for a bicycle ride, because no other child had visited, and her little boy was lonely here in England where they found it so hard to communicate. While Ram pumped up his bicycle tires, she prepared them a little picnic. Francis sat and waited in a room that smelled pleasantly of curry, and tried, unsuccessfully, to make Tara smile at him.

Then they were off, pedaling along the grassy edge of the great main road that led southward from the city and out toward the open country. Francis knew the way for he had been there once or twice with his step-father.

"Where are we going?" asked Ram, his black eyes sparkling.

"To the river," shouted Francis, forging ahead.

2

The River

They turned off the main road after about a mile and coasted along a country lane toward a picturesque village with old beamed cottages and a blacksmith's shop on a small village green. They stopped to buy pop and then cycled across the bridge to find a nice place for a picnic. The big river had risen almost to flood level, but there was a smaller tributary farther on, away from the village, where they could amuse themselves privately. Francis was not quite sure how to reach it, but he pedaled on and Ram followed trustfully. They turned into a gate that did not say Private, hid their bicycles behind the hedge, and trotted up a path that led to the top of a hill.

"I think the river is down the other side," said Francis. "Hurry up, Ram."

It was a lovely place. Great beeches with gray forked boughs arched the path, perfect for climbing. The leaves were not yet sprouting, but catkins pranced above the undergrowth, and the birds were already chattering and trilling about mating and nesting. The air was full of sunshine, life, and pollen, and Francis flung out his arms like the wings of a plane and made off down the hill as fast as he could run.

"There's the river," he shouted. "I told you so! Race me down to the bridge, Ram."

But Ram was not used to steep muddy paths. He caught his foot in a rabbit hole and fell on his nose. Being a brave and polite little boy he got up and apologized, but he was plainly worried about the mud on his trousers. "We go home soon?" he inquired hopefully.

"Home!" yelled Francis. "Not on your life! Look, I told you I knew where the river was. Come on, Ram. Step on it!"

"Why go river?" protested Ram. "De water cold and I no swim." But he followed obediently toward the bridge. They sat on a log and ate their picnic while the golden water, at flood level, hurried past, swirling round the trunks of the alders. Francis munched his sandwich and thought that this was the most wonderful afternoon he had ever experienced. Wendy and his stepfather seemed very far away and unimportant. He was free to do what he liked and to go where he pleased, and the river itself was only the beginning of adventure.

He looked around. Behind him was a sloping field where black and white cows grazed. Beyond it was a farmhouse with a barn and other buildings, and beyond that, light soil sowed with young wheat and a spring sky with white clouds scudding across it. Then he turned to look at the river, and as he did so, the sun came out, sparkling on the celandines and coltsfoot on the bank and glistening on the water.

He jumped up and ran to an alder whose trunk sloped out far over the river. His next adventure would be to scramble up it and look down on the current, but when he reached the roots he suddenly saw another adventure so dangerous and exciting that he gave a little cry of mingled fear and joy, and Ram got up and came and stood beside him.

They were looking down at a little inlet, roofed over and well hidden, where a small boat had been beached and tied to a post. But the flood had lifted it so that it rocked on a backwater—a shabby little dinghy waiting for its spring coat of paint. Francis was down the bank in a moment and sitting in it. The oars had been removed and there was no rudder. It was just a little toy craft for children to jump in and out of on a hot summer day. But to Francis it was an adventure to end all adventures. He was already working at the knots and shouting at Ram to get in.

Ram stood in the mud, tense with fear and indecision. He realized at once that to launch the little boat was exceedingly dangerous, but he knew, too, that he was quite incapable of controlling Francis, and that he could not desert him. He made one last appeal.

"No, Francis," he cried, spreading out his hands in supplication. "Come back—not good—I no swim—*Francis*!"

For the last knot had slipped, and the boat, çaught on a sideways swirl of water, was heading for the main river. Ram, who dreaded being left alone more than anything else, made a jump for it and landed in the boat beside Francis. It rocked alarmingly but held to its course. In another moment they had left the backwater behind them and were launched suddenly into midstream.

Francis fell silent, and his face grew rather pale. He had never dreamed of anything like this happening. He had imagined himself holding onto the boughs

of trees at the edge of the river and going for a nice
little ride, but the boat was now completely out of
control. It pitched along through the foaming current. Ram behind him was sobbing and muttering,
sure that his last hour had come, and Francis rather
thought it had too. He clung to the side and tried to
think, but the boat was moving so fast that he could
not think at all. If only he could steer it shoreward
and catch hold of a branch or bump into a reed island—but he could not do anything, only cling.

Then above the rush of water he heard shouting—
loud frightened shouting—from the bank. He glanced
round and saw a man—a very large, angry man—
running as fast as he could with two little boys running behind, followed by a furiously barking sheep
dog.

"The dam's just ahead, you little idiots," yelled the
angry man. "Turn the boat in! Trail your coats on
the right side."

He was running faster than the boat and had gotten
well ahead of them. Then the smaller boy clasped the
hand of the older boy, who clung to some rope or belt
tied around the middle of the angry man, who plunged
into the river in all his clothes, reminding Francis of
a furious hippopotamus.

"Can you swim?" bellowed the angry man.

"I can—he can't," yelled Francis.

"Then jump," shouted the angry man, thrashing the
water with his arms. "The dam's just ahead. *Jump,*
I tell you."

Francis glanced ahead and, sure enough, the river
seemed to disappear with a roar. Ram saw it too, gave
a loud squeal, and jumped. The angry man caught
him and held him fast.

"Pull," he shouted to the boys on the bank. "And you—hang on."

There was a great splash and a struggle. Francis seemed to swallow the river and go down to the bottom. Then he surfaced and found his hands being guided onto the dog leash, and he was being pulled ashore. The angry man was already struggling out of the water with Ram in his arms, and a moment later Francis was picked up like a drowned puppy and thrown on the grass, soaked, frozen, and sobbing.

3

The Farm

The boat had disappeared over the dam, and the little boys and the dog were racing after it, but the angry man shouted at them, very loudly, to come back. "We'll get it later," he yelled. "Take these boys to the house and tell Mum to get them warm and dry. They'll catch their deaths! Run, all of you! Stop that noise, you two, and get going. *Run,* I said."

He sounded so angry that Francis and Ram did not hesitate for a second. Coughing, gulping, and breathless they struggled to their feet and followed their swift, excited little guides. Shoes squelching, sodden clothes weighing them down, they stumbled across the field, tripping over tufts, slipping in cowpats, but never stopping for a moment because the angry man was coming along behind them, and they were more afraid of him than they had ever been afraid of anything else in their lives.

And just when they felt they were going to collapse, they made it. They crossed a yard, and the older boy held the door open, and a woman stood in the entrance, listening, while both her sons told her all about it at once as fast as they could go.

"How very, very naughty," said the woman, fairly coolly. "And what a mercy you weren't both drowned. Turn the bath on, Martin, and get in at once, both of

17

you. Kate, rinse out their clothes and put them
through the spin dryer, and they'll just have to wait till
they're dry. I'll find some old things, and they can sit
by the fire. Now, hurry up, you naughty boys—get
along upstairs!"

About quarter of an hour later they were sitting
by the kitchen fire, sipping hot mugs of tea, Francis
in a robe and pajamas rather too small for him and
Ram in a similar outfit much too big for him. The
angry man was by now snorting and splashing in the
bath, and they both hoped that he would stay there
for a long, long time. Kate, a girl of about fifteen,
glanced at them rather scornfully as she spread out
their clothes to dry in front of the blaze and marched
away with a backward toss of her long, fair hair.

But to Martin and Chris, the farmer's sons, they
were heroes, for the fact that they had only just escaped being drowned made them wonderful adven-
turers. The four boys sat on the hearthrug, and Francis described their perilous journey in a whisper with
one eye on the kitchen door, in case the angry man
appeared. And as he told it, it grew more and more
perilous, and his listeners' eyes grew rounder and
rounder. He was just beginning to wonder whether
he dare introduce a crocodile, when the woman came
in.

"Now, come along," she said. "Your clothes are
fairly dry now, and you must be getting home. What
are your names and where do you live and how did
you get here?"

Francis looked at Ram. Perhaps these people would
tell the police, and perhaps they could give the wrong
address, but as Ram would never think of it, it was
no good. So they both gave the details meekly enough

and explained that they had come on bicycles, which were hidden behind a hedge near the main road.

The woman glanced out of the window. Already the sky was orange behind the bare elm branches.

"It's just about sunset," she remarked. "Have you got lights? You're a long way from home."

They shook their heads. They had never cycled in the dark before.

"Well, perhaps your parents had better come and fetch you," suggested the woman. "Do you have a phone?"

"Ram doesn't," said Francis quickly, "and my dad goes out on Saturday evening, and Mum couldn't leave my little sisters. P'raps we could walk."

"So dark," murmured Ram, and Francis, as he turned to him, saw the fear and misery in his huge black eyes. If the angry man got anywhere near Ram's father, Ram would be punished in true Indian style. He was even more afraid of his father than he was of the dark, so he added tremblingly, "Us walk quick now!"

Just then the door opened, and the angry man came into the room. But clad in dry clothes and no longer out of breath, he looked less angry. He listened to the problem and made up his mind at once.

"I'll run them back in the Landrover and pick up their bikes on the way," he said. "I'd like a word with their parents. They should know what their boys are doing."

Francis glanced at Ram again.

"You oughtn't to go to Ram's father," he said loudly and boldly. "It wasn't Ram's fault. He didn't want to go. He was afraid of being left alone, and I told him to jump in."

The angry man, who was really the farmer, looked steadily at Francis. His face was grave, but he was not angry any longer.

"I'd guessed as much," he said quite kindly. "We'll give him another chance. But you—whatever made you do a fool thing like that? And do your parents know where you are?"

Francis shook his head.

"Mum's in bed with a headache," he muttered, "and Dad went out with my sisters—and he's not my dad anyway—he doesn't care what I do." The old chorus was starting up again, and he nearly said, "It isn't fair!" but he stopped himself in time. After all, it was no business of theirs.

"I see," said the farmer quite kindly. "Well, someone seems to have been taking care of you both, or you might be lying at the bottom of the river. I'll just lock up, and then we'll get along."

He left the room, his boys behind him, and the farmer's wife started turning the clothes while Francis leaned his head against an armchair and gazed around the room. He was beginning to feel very warm and drowsy and found himself staring at a large card stuck on the wall. In ragged, uneven letters were printed the words God Is Luv.

"That's spelled wrong," said Francis suddenly.

The farmer's wife smiled. "I know," she said. "Chris wrote it all by himself when he was four, for his father's birthday. It made us laugh, and we've always kept it. You see, Francis, its true however you spell it. Loving is God's way, and it's a far better way than running off and taking what doesn't belong to you. Now these are dry—get into them."

They dressed by the kitchen fire. The farmer's wife

piled on more logs, and the flames leaped up afresh. Kate was setting the table, and there was a delicious smell of bread baking. Francis longed to stay, but there was nothing to stay for. The farmer returned and told them to come, and his wife escorted them to the door.

" 'Bye, boys," she said, "and don't you ever do a silly thing like that again. Thank God you're both safe!" She smiled into their upturned faces and laid her hands for an instant on their hair. A moment later they were climbing into the Landrover, and Francis, looking back through the window, could see Martin and Chris squatting by the fire, laughing, while clear on the wall above them stood out the words that seemed to embody the spirit of the house, God Is Luv. Then the engine started up, and the window was hidden behind the barn.

They dropped Ram and his bicycle at the end of the street, and he scuttled home without a backward look, while Francis pressed a little closer to the farmer. Somehow, he did not want to say good-bye to this big man who had appeared at that moment of terror and saved him, who was not angry any longer, and who had understood completely that it was not Ram's fault. The farmer too was driving more slowly, as though uncertain of what to do.

"That's my house," said Francis rather sadly.

"Is it?" said the farmer, drawing up at the roadside. But he did not move. "Why on earth did you do such a silly thing as that, Francis?" he said at last. "You nearly drowned that poor little Indian. You knew he couldn't swim, and, besides, it was stealing. It wasn't your boat. Your parents should know about it, or you may do something like that again."

Francis said nothing. He just climbed out of the
Landrover, lifted out his bicycle, and led the farmer
in through the back door.

The kitchen was in an awful mess. No one had
cleared the table or washed the dishes. His mother's
voice, tearful and angry, called sharply from the top
of the stairs. "Francis, where have you been? How
dare you stay out so late! I shall tell your Dad when
he comes in, and you deserve all you'll get."

"He won't come in till midnight, not on Saturday
he won't," whispered Francis. "And she won't tell
him nothing, 'cause he's usually drunk."

"I see," said the farmer, looking around thoughtfully. He squatted down beside the boy and looked
deep into his eyes.

"Promise you won't do silly things like that anymore."

"Promise."

"And come and see us again."

"Promise."

The huge hand pressed his shoulder and a moment
later the farmer was gone, leaving Francis standing
irresolute in the kitchen, fighting back his tears. It had
been a very big, important day for him, but now he
felt tired, cold, and desolate. He had run away and
tasted freedom. He had nearly been drowned. He
had also had a glimpse of something-that-might-have-
been—a glimpse of a firelit home where everyone
seemed happy and of anger that was both just and
kind and did not make him feel angry in return. He
longed to run to his mother and tell her all about it,
and he seemed in luck, for Wendy and Debby were
sitting in front of the television absorbed in a film.

He ran upstairs. She had been lying down, and the

bedclothes were thrown back, but she was sitting on
the bed clasping and unclasping her hands. She had
been very anxious about him, but now that he was
safely home, the sight of him standing there looking
so pleased with himself merely annoyed her.

"I don't know how you can be so selfish, Francis,"
she burst out. "You knew how worried I'd be. Don't
you *care*? Where have you been anyway?"

"Out on my bike, Mum. I fell into the river and
the river's flooded and I nearly went over the dam,
but a man pulled me out. Mum, I nearly got
drowned."

Her face went rather pale. "You've no business
to go anywhere near the river," she snapped at him.
"And I believe you're making all this up, anyway.
Your clothes look perfectly dry and clean. It's very
naughty indeed of you, Francis."

"But Mum, the lady put them into the spin dryer,
and we sat by the fire—and I did nearly drown, honest
Mum. The man said so—he brought me home in
his Landrover and—"

A car drew up outside. She leaped to her feet and
ran eagerly to the window and peered out. A moment
later she spoke again.

"I thought it was your dad," she said in a dull flat
voice, "but it's for the house next door."

She did not come back. She stood staring down the
road, still clasping and unclasping her hands. She had
forgotten all about Francis and the river.

He waited for a moment and then turned away.
He went into the living room, gave Wendy a good
pinch, clasped his hand over her mouth to shut her
up, and settled down with her on the sofa to watch the
end of the film.

4

The Cherry Tree Again

Francis heard no more of his adventure. His mother came down late on Sunday morning looking ill and tired and seemed to have forgotten all about it. After breakfast she shut herself up in the bedroom with Dad, and their voices grew very loud. When she came out she looked as though she had been crying. Dad was in a bad mood, and the little girls were fussing. Francis made himself scarce.

Out in the yard things were better. Fluffy clouds scudded across a blue sky, and two daffodil buds had opened right out and turned into daffodils. Birds sang everywhere, and it was impossible to feel dull. Things were shooting up out of the damp soil so fast that you could almost see them coming.

He kicked his football around for a time, but the lawn was very small. He looked thoughtfully towards the gate, and then he stiffened and stared very hard indeed, for something peculiar had happened to the gate. There were ten brown knuckles arranged along the top of it, and two very bright black eyes peered through the crack. Someone was watching.

Francis knew who it was at once, and he was glad. Ram was not much of a footballer, but he was better than nobody, and he had not made a fuss or blamed

Francis even when he had nearly gotten drowned. It would be fun to talk over their great adventure, and because they had nearly died together, Francis decided to show him the hiding place in the cherry tree. He went and opened the gate just a chink. Ram slipped inside and looked at him with shining eyes.

"I come, Francis," he whispered, glancing nervously at the house. "You well? Your Mum, she cross?"

"Not really," said Francis. "I don't think she really believed me. My clothes were too clean. Ram, there's a secret place where I go. I'll take you if you like, but you mustn't tell anyone ever. No one knows about it 'cept me."

Ram looked startled. Yesterday Francis had led him into terrible trouble, and he did not want it to happen again. He hesitated, but Francis seized his hand.

"Come on, Ram," he urged, "it isn't dangerous. It's a tree. And hurry 'cause I don't want anyone to see us. Creep behind that laurel hedge and run across the grass. Now quick, climb!"

Ram, quite relieved that he was not expected to disappear down a subterranean tunnel, climbed up nimbly enough, with Francis after him. It was a tight fit, but they managed and sat there pressed together peering through the swelling twigs. "We shall soon be completely hidden by cherry blossom," said Francis. "It will be like white curtains all round us. Look, Ram. There's Mrs. Glengarry putting all her cats out before she goes to church. She can't see us. She doesn't know we're here. But we can see her. We can see everything!"

He laughed out loud, and Ram laughed too. The

tree swayed slightly in the spring breeze, and somewhere behind them church bells were ringing. They
opened the box and spread out their treasures, and
Ram produced a packet of jelly beans out of his
pocket. They sat sucking, swinging their legs, and
reliving their adventure of the day before, and Ram
felt happier than he had ever felt since his arrival in
cold, gray England six months before.

All winter he had suffered from chilblains, and he
had never really felt warm at all. School was misery,
and he had never made a friend because he was so
small and shy, and the English language was so difficult. The others had not meant to be unkind, but
they were all in such a hurry and made such a noise
that he had never found time or a loud enough voice
to explain that he would like to play too. So he had
felt very lonely and never really safe except at home
with his mother and little sister.

But now everything was different. He was sitting
close to his new friend in the rather uncomfortable
fork of a tree, sucking jelly beans, and the birds were
singing, and the bells were ringing, and the English
sun seemed warmer than he had ever known it before.
He expanded and began to speak the English language
better than he had ever done before. There seemed
nothing he could not say in his own way. He talked
about India, the journey, the plane, and his family,
whereas Francis talked about football and all the adventures he was planning for the future.

The world seemed as bright as the daffodils and
the sunshine until Francis said, quite suddenly, "Do
you like school?"

The light died out of Ram's eyes, and he shook his
head violently.

"I not like school," he said, and looked miserable.

"Why not?" asked Francis. "It's all right. Our teacher's all right, and we play football and go swimming. What's wrong with that?"

Ram turned great tragic black eyes on him.

"I no like school," he repeated with a little shudder. "I afraid."

"Afraid? What of?"

"I afraid of Spotty and Tyke. They run after me. They say they do something bad for me."

He was whispering and peering round as though Spotty and Tyke might be hiding in the bushes, and Francis hugged himself excitedly for that sounded like the beginning of another adventure.

Spotty was a rather overgrown thirteen-year-old with pimples, hitting back at a world that made fun of his fat body and spotty face, but Tyke was something different. Tyke was strong and wiry and an excellent runner. He went about with a cigarette hanging from his lower lip, when the teachers were not looking, and drank beer, stolen from his dad. Francis thought he was wonderful and spent a great deal of time during the lunch hour trying to make Tyke notice him. Both boys lived at his end of town, and he occasionally met them in the fish-and-chips shop.

"They're all right," said Francis. "Why should they do anything to you? And, anyhow, when do they talk to you?"

Ram's eyes became even more frightened.

"They have a little house," he whispered, "near our house. One day, I pick blackberries—I not know they in little house—I hear them talk bad things, and I run away quick. Then they saw me." He shuddered.

"They run fast, fast, fast, and they take me so—" He
seized the collar of Francis's shirt. "They say they
do bad things to me if I tell—they come to my
house—they kill me if I tell."

He had worked himself up into a terrible state, and
his hands were cold and clammy. He had never told
anyone, but his whole life was blighted by the shadow
of Spotty and Tyke. The thought of them haunted
him at night, and he had nightmares in which he
imagined they were coming in at the window. He was
sure that they followed him home from school, and
once or twice they had really done so, in order to show
him that he had better look out.

And he had looked out, carrying his terrible secret
all by himself until that sunny Sunday morning when
the birdsong and the sweetness of having a friend had
made him forget his misery, and he had blurted it all
out to Francis. But Francis was safe; Francis would
never tell. He could trust Francis. He would tell him
everything forever.

Francis stared. He felt quite jealous that Tyke
should have paid so must attention to Ram. And to
think that they had a place—not far away—a secret
hideout where they probably kept knives and bombs.
It was whispered that Tyke had once started a fire,
and he had other friends beside Spotty who smoked
with him behind the gym. Perhaps they were a gang,
and Francis could do something to make them notice
him. After all, he was a very fast runner.

Somewhere near the back door, an angry voice
shouted his name, but he took no notice.

"Tell me about the hideout," he said. "Where exactly is it?"

"Down our street another street," said Ram, talk-

ing very fast, "and down end of other street fields and
blackberries. And last house in other street burned—
and behind burned house, little house not to live in.
There Tyke and Spotty and other boys go, and when
I pick blackberries I hear them, and they see me in a
little window and they say *very* bad things to me."

"Yes, yes," said Francis, who did not want to hear
that all over again. "But when do they go there?"

"I see them Sunday," said Ram, "I see Tyke and
Spotty and sometime others go along the road before
night."

"Do you mean about sunset?"

"Yes, when not dark, but soon dark. I see them
go."

"Do you see them come back?"

"No. My mother she pull the curtain."

How stupid he is, thought Francis, holding out his
hand for another jelly bean. *I should watch and watch
and clock them in and clock them out.* He was not
listening to what Ram was saying anymore. His imag-
ination was carrying him away. Tyke was waiting for
him outside the fish-and-chips shop, drawing him
aside. "Our gang needs a runner," he was saying, "a
very fast, small runner. How about it?" He suddenly
wanted to be alone to think and plan.

"I'm going in now," he said to Ram. "You'd better
go home."

Ram looked disappointed. It had been so wonderful spilling out all his fears to Francis, and, having
shared them, he felt much less afraid. But there would
be other days, plenty of other days. He scrambled to
the ground.

"I come again?" he inquired timidly.

"Maybe, some day," said Francis without looking

at him. He had almost forgotten Ram. He stuck his hands in his pockets and sauntered toward the back door. As he turned the corner of the house he nearly bumped into his stepfather, who was cleaning the car.

"Where have *you* been?" said his stepfather, irritably. "You know perfectly well you're meant to help me wash the car on Sunday morning. I've told you before."

"I was only in the yard," replied Francis, sullenly kicking the step.

"You were *not* in the yard," shouted Dad. "I searched and called everywhere. I'm sick of your lies and your laziness. It's just about lunchtime now, but this afternoon you stop right here and do what I tell you, and no nonsense!"

Francis escaped into the kitchen. His afternoon's plans were all spoiled now, and he would have to wait a whole week till next Sunday. He aimed a hard kick at a chair leg and then noticed his mother standing quite still looking out the window, her hands resting on the sink. It was as though she was watching something so intently that she had never even heard him come in.

They were quite alone, and she was quiet and not busy. If he went to her now and told her about the house in the cherry tree, then one day when Dad and Wendy and Debby were out in the park and the blossoms were out in the tree, he would take the stepladder, and she would come and sit with him in a secret white world. It would be rather crowded, but he could sit higher up. He would buy some mints, and they would talk, just she and he, like they used to long ago when Wendy was still quite a baby, before Mummy started getting headaches, and before Dad started going out all the time and being so cross. If that happened, then he would not bother about Tyke and Spotty. He would stay at home and be good and help her. He took a step toward her.

"Mum," he whispered.

She turned with a start, and the sight of him standing there, with smears of green bark all down his clean jersey, irritated her beyond endurance. If he had behaved himself her husband would have been in quite a good humor by now. It was always Francis who upset him, and the little wretch did not seem to care at all. He was grinning at her as though he had done something clever.

"What are you creeping up behind me and making me jump like that for?" she said angrily. "And where on earth have you been? You know perfectly well you are meant to help your father on Sunday mornings. You—you just spoil everything, Francis! Now for goodness sake, go and wash your hands and don't start a row during lunch. He's here little enough as it is!"

Something seemed to snap in her, and she turned to the oven with a little sob. Francis fled from the room. The fragile, white world of the cherry tree had vanished, and he knew that he would join a gang as soon as possible—a really bad gang that blew things up and hurt people. He wanted to start right away, but the only victim in sight was Whiskers, his own tabby cat that he had had since she was a kitten. She purred at the sight of him, but he ran at her and kicked her out into the yard as hard as he could, then slammed the door on her squeal of pain and fear.

5

The Gang

One result of happenings of that Sunday morning was that Ram became Francis's faithful little shadow. He waited to go to school with him, followed him about all day, and longed for another invitation to come and sit in the cherry tree. But it never came. Francis quite enjoyed Ram's admiration, and he liked the little presents Ram brought him, but he found him a bit of a bore when his other friends were around and usually could not be bothered with him. But Ram was unoffended and put Francis's coldness down to English manners, which were quite different from Indian manners and were something you had to get used to, like the English food and weather and always being in a hurry.

Besides, Francis had a great deal to think about. He had followed Tyke and Spotty at lunch hour and strolled past their hideout as though by mistake, just when they were enjoying their daily smoke. They had seized him and threatened him with terrible punishments and a beating if he told on them, but he assured them that he was just starting to smoke himself and would be delighted to join them. He then tried to buy a pack of cigarettes, but the lady in the shop refused to sell to him. So he collected his father's stubs, went up the cherry tree to experiment, and was very

sick into Mrs. Glengarry's yard. It seemed a losing
battle.

But at least they had noticed him, and they knew
that, although he was so much younger, he was on
their side, and that encouraged him. When Sunday
came around again, he took no risks. He cleaned and
rubbed the car till it shone, and his stepfather praised
him, and his mother told him, rather absent-mindedly,
that he was a good boy. She was unable to concentrate on anything that morning because she was not
sure whether Dad was going to stay home that afternoon and take them out, or not.

"Do you want to come, Francie, if Dad has time
to take us?" she asked. "You usually feel sick in the
car, don't you, so don't bother if you'd rather stay.
We shan't be long, and we'll bring something nice for
tea."

She doesn't really want me to come, thought Francis. *She thinks I'll say something and make Dad mad
or fight Wendy in the back. I don't want to go anyhow.* Aloud he said, "I'll stay here, Mum. I don't
like the car much. Take Wendy and Deb. I want to
do things by myself."

His mother laughed at his important-sounding voice
and kissed him.

She was happy that afternoon. The sun was shining, the birds were singing, her husband was in a good
mood and had decided to take her and the girls to the
amusement park. It would be a much more peaceful
afternoon if Francis stayed at home, for Wendy and
Debby hardly ever quarreled, and both got along well
with their father. It was a great relief that Francis did
not want to come.

Francis watched them go, waving to him, and was

surprised at the queer, lonely feeling inside him. He wanted to belong somewhere, and he knew that he did not really belong inside that car. But now was his great chance to belong to Tyke's gang, and he must escape quickly in case Ram came to visit. He stuck his two-bladed knife in his pocket and set off at a run. He did not suppose they would be there so early in the afternoon, but he would just snoop around and have a look.

He knew exactly where to go. The house was the last one in the road, and beyond it was a hedge and a playing field. An old woman had lived there, and one night she had accidentally set her house afire. She had run out screaming and was now in an Old People's Home. The blaze had been quenched, but a lot of damage had been done. So far, the city had done nothing about it, and it remained blackened and empty, with the windows boarded up.

Francis had never been through the gate before. Once inside the yard, his heart began to beat very fast indeed, and he realized that he was not very brave. What if he joined the gang and they made him do scary, dangerous things in the dark? He suddenly wanted to run home to his mother. It must be nearly teatime, and they were bringing something nice for tea. Then he remembered that they had not really wanted him. They liked best to be just the four of them, and here in the gang he might really and truly belong and become an important person. His fear gave place to excitement, and he peeped around the corner of the house. At the back there was an old toolshed with a door on one hinge, which did not shut properly. He could slip inside without even opening it.

It was a horrible place—empty cans, bottles, and cigarette ends littered the floor, the walls were mildewed, and the windows stuffed with rags. There were some old bits of matting, a bench, a broken chair, a tin box containing tools and knives, a candle and matches, and a pile of paperbacks on the shelf. Francis thumbed through them, enjoying the cover pictures of blazing tanks, murdered ladies, crashing planes, or one-eyed monsters from space, but the stories were too old for him, and he soon put them back.

A smelly, sordid place it was, but to Francis it seemed the very gate of Paradise! He sat for a long time daydreaming and forgot all about teatime. Then he went outside to the little patch of yard behind the shed, and even he thought how wretched it looked—a trampled piece of earth covered with rotten cabbages and rusty cans. There was an old rake leaning against the wall, and he set to work collecting the rubbish. The birds had stopped singing and shadows lay across the yard, but it was nowhere near sunset. There was still time.

He worked on, still daydreaming. Perhaps they would be pleased that he had cleaned up the yard. Perhaps if he dug up the earth he could grow mustard and cress and radishes and make sandwiches for Tyke. He had done it before at home and had made sandwiches for Mum. The sky above the hedge was crimson now, but he did not want to leave before he had finished his job.

And then, quite suddenly, they came.

They charged into the shed and lit the lantern, which shone out through the gap in the door, making a broad beam across the path. To escape, he would

have to cross that beam, so he crouched behind a
bramble, pressed himself against the wall, and waited.
There were three of them, and he could hear everything they said and the rasp of matches and the opening of cans. They were smoking, and they seemed to
be making some sort of plan. "A little walk round"
they called it, and Francis learned that the telephone
booth outside Ram's house was doing no one any
good and why not smash it?

He crouched, trembling and listening, and wondering what to do. They might stay there for hours
and Mum would be crying and Dad hopping mad,
but he dared not move, for this was not the introduc-
tion he had imagined. What if they found him in the
dark and murdered him in cold blood before he had
time to explain himself? Spotty would be scared to
do a thing like that, but Tyke would stop at nothing.
Tyke was wonderful! Francis's heart glowed with admiration, and then quite suddenly, because the March
night was cold, he sneezed.

He heard the boys leap to their feet, and then there
was dead silence, and Francis wondered for a moment
whether they were quite so brave as he had imagined.
At last Tyke opened the door very cautiously indeed.
"Bet it's that little Wog!" he whispered uncertainly.

"Not him!" quavered Spotty. "We scared the day-
lights out of him."

"Who's there?" said Tyke.

They seemed to be coming nearer, all together, and
Francis realized, with a thrill of terror, that his only
hope was to give himself up. They might do anything
to him if they found him crouching in the dark.

He rose up from behind the bramble, and they all
sprang back using words Francis had never heard be-

fore. But when they saw how small he was, standing alone in the light, they came forward and dragged him into the shed. They pinched him and slapped him, but not very hard, and he did not really mind, for this was his big test. This was his initiation into manhood.

"What did you hear?" demanded Tyke, holding his wrists and looking at him with narrowed eyes.

"I heard about the phone booth," blurted out Francis. "And Tyke, let me join your gang! If you want to smash phone booths, I could help you. I can run ever so fast—I'm the fastest under eleven in the school. I could watch out and warn you, and you could smash anything you wanted."

" 'Tyke' indeed! 'Thomas Isaacs' from you, if you don't mind!" But he stared thoughtfully into those bright, intelligent eyes lifted to his. They showed no fear, only a sort of adoration, and Tyke, who had known very little love or admiration in his life, felt rather queer. He had always dreamed of being a kind of brigand chief, but his only followers so far were fat Spotty and Bonkers, who was supposed to be a little bit wrong in the head and was about to be transferred to a special school. He was getting rather tired of both of them, but this one was different. He could teach this one anything and make what he liked of him. Besides, if he had really overheard them, he had better be watched. There had been some other acts of vandalism, and the police were on the lookout. So he squeezed Francis's wrists a little harder.

"Right," he said fiercely. "You can do some running for us. You're not to hang round us at school, see? We don't want you. But you can come here next Sunday at this time, and we'll teach you a thing or two. Ever smoked?"

"Yes," said Francis eagerly, and forbore to mention how sick he had been.

"And—if—you—tell—on—us—" Tyke's eyes narrowed again. He pushed his face close to Francis's and uttered such awful blood-curdling threats that Francis shivered. But he was not really afraid because he would never, never tell, not on pain of death.

"Right," said Tyke again. "All ready? Now listen, and don't you dare make a mistake! Run to the end of the road by the T-junction and stand against the wall. Look right and left. When no one's coming either way, step out under the street light and raise your hand. D'you get me?"

"Mmm," breathed Francis.

"Right—now, scram!"

Francis scrammed. He thought he had never run so fast before, for Tyke was watching him, and that seemed to lend wings to his feet. He pressed himself against the wall, invisible in his gray jersey, and peered round the corner. A car was coming. It turned into the road where he stood and drew up outside a house. That was most unfortunate. But what was even more unfortunate was that it was his dad's car, and Dad sat inside tooting softly on the horn.

Francis's eyes grew larger and larger. If his dad turned and came back, the car lights would shine right on him. It would be safest to run home quickly, but faithfulness to Tyke kept him rooted to the spot, and a moment later the door of the house opened, and a lady in very high heels came clicking down the path. Dad leaned over, opened the car door, and started up the engine. They drove straight on and turned down a side street while Francis gave a great sigh of relief. He peeped round the corner again, and there was no one coming at all. He stepped into the lamplight and raised his hand, and he felt it was the most glorious thing he had ever done.

And as he raised it the three dark forms began running, their feet noiseless on the grass. As they reached the telephone booth they became a dark, confused mass. Francis heard the tinkle of broken glass and saw the light go out. It was over in a few seconds, and they sped on past him, still standing, fascinated, under the light.

"Go home, you little fool," ordered Tyke, turning to the left while Spotty and Bonkers sped to the right. Francis saw a couple of doors open and realized why they were in such a hurry. He too turned and fled and did not stop running till he reached his home. He was very thankful that his father was out. Tea had been cleared away, and he felt hungry. He was just peering hopefully into the pantry when his mother came in.

"Francis," she said sharply, "tea is over, and if you can't come home in time you need not have any. There's a glass of milk and a slice of bread, and then you're to go straight to bed. Where have you been anyway?"

"Just playing in the next street," he muttered sullenly, shuffling his feet.

"Well, I don't know what you think you're doing in the next street at this hour. Your father's really cross about it. He's just gone out, but tomorrow you're going to catch it, and you deserve all you get."

Francis was very hungry indeed, and he suddenly thought of a way to distract his mother's attention. He stuck his hands in his pockets and looked up at her.

"I know he's gone out," he said. "I saw him."

"Rubbish! You said you were playing in the next street. How could you have seen him?"

"But he came into the next street. He stopped outside a house and tooted."

"And what happened?"

"A lady came out and got into the car, and they drove away."

Her eyes seemed to be boring holes in him. Her face was very white and her voice very quiet.

"What was the lady like?"

"Kind of fat with yellow hair—I couldn't see much."

"Francis, are you making all this up? You seem to have been telling a lot of lies lately."

"It's true. Honest, Mum. I'll show you the house."

But she had turned away, clenching her hands. She had forgotten all about him. He walked straight into the pantry and helped himself to bread, butter, ham, a large slice of apple tart, and a glass of milk. Then he hurried up to his bedroom and settled down to enjoy his supper. He was feeling utterly, recklessly happy. It had been great fun watching them smash that telephone booth, and Tyke was a wonderful leader. And he, Francis, belonged. He was important. They had seen how fast he could run—they had accepted him.

He climbed into bed and lay thinking of the rosy, grabbing, smashing future ahead of him. He was just falling asleep when there was a tiny noise at the windowsill, and Whiskers jumped onto his bed. He lifted the blankets, and she crept in beside him and curled herself into a warm ball against his chest. He stroked her thoughtfully and felt rather sad.

It was no fun at all kicking Whiskers. She was much too forgiving. She only loved and purred.

6

The Fire

He awoke in the night to a confused noise of Daddy shouting and Mum crying, but he fell asleep almost immediately and wondered in the morning if it had all been a dream. But somehow from then onward things seemed to go from bad to worse at home. Dad was nearly always out, and Mum seemed to have gone to pieces. She would scream at Wendy and slap Debby when they had not been particularly naughty, and kiss and hug them when they had not been particularly good. It was more than Francis could cope with, and he kept out of the way as much as possible.

But school was wonderful that Monday morning. Not that Tyke took any notice of him, or that he so much as glanced in Tyke's direction. He knew his place and played with his own friends, but there was an invisible sense of comradeship, and it seemed glorious even to be sharing the same playground. Besides, it was only six days to next Sunday.

On Tuesday evening he dared to saunter round and look at the damage—the glass was shattered, the receiver broken, and the connection cut through with wirecutters. The place looked a shambles, and he was feeling a glow of pride at his own part in such a satisfactory job, when Ram, whose house was just

opposite, saw him and came hurrying out. He thought
Francis had come to visit him, and his small brown
face was alight with joy. Francis, who liked chapati,
let the mistake pass and followed him into his living
room.

Ram's father was there, and he too seemed pleased
to see Francis. He spoke English quite well. "We are
going to a parent-teacher meeting at the school from
seven thirty to eight thirty," he explained. "Tara is
in bed, and Ram will be all alone. Could you not
come and play with him, and you can buy fish and
chips for supper at the corner shop? I will take you
home about nine."

Francis thought that a very good idea, although he
did wonder for a moment why his own parents were
not going to the school meeting. He quite liked Ram
when there was no one more interesting about, and he
had some really good toys. Also, Francis loved fish
and chips.

"I'll ask my mother," he said and darted off, and
his mother, as he expected, was quite relieved to know
for once where he was and to have him safely out of
the way. He was getting more and more quarrelsome
and difficult at home, and the little girls became quite
unmanageable when he was about. Besides, she had
a headache coming on.

Once the parents had left, he and Ram settled down
to a complicated game of armies on the rug. They
arranged regiments all over the room and knocked
them down with marbles. It was nice and warm with
the gas fire on, and they pushed the sofa towards the
wall to make more room for their game. After a while
they felt hungry and set out for the fish-and-chips shop
at the corner.

It was only a few minutes away, but there was a line, and they took some time deciding whether they wanted fish or hot pies. They trotted home under the stars, chatting and eating chips, but as they opened the front door they recoiled in horror. Clouds of gray smoke billowed from the house, knocking them backwards.

Ram grasped the situation first. "It's the sofa," he screamed. "Too near the fire. Francis, phone the police and fire engine—999. My father told me, always 999—I get Tara."

He dashed for the staircase but was driven back, blind and choking. Three times he tried and then knew it was impossible. He gazed at the window; it was shut. As yet he could see no flames, only suffocating smoke. He must call the neighbors, and surely the fire engine would be here in a moment! He looked round wildly and realized that the telephone booth was wrecked and the city, as yet, had done nothing about it.

Francis too had remembered as he turned, and the thought had struck him like lightning: *So this is the price of wrecking a phone booth—little Tara's life, perhaps.* And he had been so proud of his part in it. But it was only a passing thought, for there was no time to lose. He banged on the door of the nearest house, but the occupants were out. He knocked at the next, but they had no telephone, although they ran out to help. It was clearly no good wasting time. Perhaps none of these little houses had telephones. He had better run home. His mother would know what to do.

Never before had he run so fast. Last time he had run, Tyke had been watching him, but now it was

little Tara's life at stake. He ran under that glorious
street light, but the glory had departed. He arrived
home completely out of breath, but his mother
smelled the smoke at once and rushed to the telephone as he gasped out a few words. "Fire engine and
ambulance, seventy-five Draper Street," she shouted,
"and there's a child in an upstairs bedroom that they
can't reach."

She suddenly seemed immensely strong, swift, and
capable, and Francis wondered if he had ever really
known his mother before tonight. "The ladder, Francis," she cried. "It's in the garage. Take one end and
I'll take the other—don't talk—run—no Wendy, you
can't come. Go back to bed at once."

He had certainly never known that his mother could
run so fast. He could hardly keep up with her. This
was a wonderful run, he and his mother together, to
save a life. But as they turned the corner they saw
that the neighbors were already coping and had turned
their garden hoses onto the blaze. Only their ladders were too short, and already flames were leaping
in the house. The smoldering sofa was ablaze, and
the curtains had caught. One neighbor in particular
seemed to have taken charge.

"Hurry up," he shouted. "Keep the hoses on. The
ceiling will go in a minute. Give me your belts or
suspenders—anything to tie these ladders together—
the girl's in the front room, he says—got a hammer
and a wet towel, mate? I'll have to break the glass."

Everyone was running in and out of houses, helping, bringing what was needed, and the joined ladders
were just being hoisted when Francis and his mother
appeared. The neighbor shinned up, and there was a
crash of falling glass. He fumbled for the catch but

drew back, blinded by the smoke.

"I can't see the bed," he shouted down. "Where is it?"

"I show you," shrieked Ram. He clambered up the ladder like a monkey and pitched himself through the window after the man. Holding his breath and with eyes shut, he guided him to the bed where Tara lay, huddled under the bedclothes, limp and helpless. The man picked her up and slung her over his shoulder. Now that the window was open the smoke was less dense.

"Get her into the fresh air first," gasped the man, clambering out. "Now come on, son, keep it up. You can take a breath now."

They all seemed to slide down the ladder together and collapse on the ground. Eager hands took Tara and laid her on a rug on the pavement. Ram was covered with blood for he had fallen onto the broken glass, and his face and hands were badly cut, but he hardly seemed to notice. He took some great breaths of fresh air and struggled over to where Tara lay, with a little group of women kneeling round her. One of them was giving her artificial respiration.

"She alive?" gasped Ram.

"I don't know, dear," said Francis's mother, putting her arms round the sooty, bloody little figure. "I think so—I hope so. The engine and the ambulance should be here by now, but of course there was that delay in phoning."

"It was wicked, messing up the phone booth like that," murmured another woman. "May have cost the kiddie her life."

At that point they heard the blessed sound, the high, sirenlike wails of the fire engine and the ambu-

lance, and everybody stood back as the men rushed
into action.

But Francis hardly noticed the fire fighters. His
eyes were fixed on the limp little figure that was Tara,
and just as they were lifting her into the ambulance
and fixing up the oxygen mask, her parents came
walking down the street from the bus stop.

Francis's mother ran to meet them and steered
Tara's dazed mother in beside the stretcher. "You'd
better take Ram too," she said. "He's dreadfully cut."

She turned to the father, who was weeping and
beating his breast. "Who has a car," she asked, "and
could take Tara's dad to the hospital?"

Several volunteers stepped forward, eager to help,
and as the bewildered man climbed into a car, she
laid her hand on his shoulder. "When you come
back," she said, "come straight to our house for a
meal. Twenty-three Graham Avenue. We'll expect
you any time of the day or night."

"What'll Dad say about them coming?" asked Francis as they walked home with the ladder. "He doesn't
like immigrants."

"He can say what he likes," said his mother shortly.
"That was a very, very brave little boy, Francis. You
ought to be proud to have such a friend."

They put the ladder away and made themselves tea
and sandwiches at the kitchen table. They had stayed
to watch the firemen get the blaze under control, and
it was quite late. The little girls were asleep, and Dad
was still out. Francis, shaken more deeply than he
realized by his part in what had happened, sat very
close to his mother.

"How did it start, Francis?" she asked, sipping her
tea.

"I don't know. We were at the fish-and-chip shop. I think Ram pushed the sofa too near the gas fire, 'cause we were playing a game. Mum, d'you think Tara's dead?"

"I don't think so. Her heart was beating. Pray God, she'll be all right!"

"What good does praying do, Mum?"

"I'm not sure. I used to think it helped—nothing seems to help anymore. I wish you went to Sunday school, Francis—I wish you could all grow up good— I don't know what to do!"

Her tears were falling into her teacup, and Francis flung his arms round her and clung to her. Without knowing it, he had learned many new things that night: the price of destruction, the beauty of courage, the value of life. And now, held close in his mother's arms, he suddenly knew where he really belonged. "I'll try to be good," he whispered, "but Wendy does pinch first."

Tyke's rule was tottering.

7

In Trouble

But of course it was not quite as easy as that, because Tyke had no intention of letting go. Francis in his power might be an asset, but Francis loose was dangerous. He knew far too much. So when he did not turn up on Sunday afternoon, Tyke wanted to know why.

"Hi, you, come behind the gym," he ordered on Monday morning and stalked ahead with the younger boy trotting behind. When they got there, Tyke turned and seized Francis's wrists rather painfully and glared down at him. He noticed that the answering look of adoration was no longer there.

"How come you weren't there last night?" he demanded.

"My dad wouldn't let me," lied Francis, but then he realized that excuse would not do every week, so he blurted out, "You know, Tyke—I mean, Isaacs—I don't want to bash up any more phone booths. When Ram's house caught on fire, Tara, his little sister, got trapped upstairs, and I couldn't phone 'cause it was bashed up. I had to run home, and the fire engine didn't come for ages, and Tara nearly died. You wouldn't like your little sister to die, would you, 'cause the phone booth was bashed up?"

Tyke, being the only child of a broken marriage, shrugged his shoulders, but he had the sense to realize that he had gone too fast. If he wanted to make this boy like himself, he would have to go more gently. He spoke quite kindly.

"Right," he said. "No more phone booths! You come along next Sunday, and we'll have some nice quiet fun, just the four of us. And if you tell—"

"I'll never tell, Tyke—I mean, Isaacs—cross my heart, I'll never tell anyone."

Tyke narrowed his eyes and repeated his threats in a low voice, and Francis nodded and ran off. But the child had changed, and Tyke felt a queer sense of loss. He smoked a cigarette, and when Spotty came to join him, he told him to get out because he was sick to death of him.

But Francis was happy, happier than he had been for a long time. Tara had not died. She had probably been cuddled down so far under the bedclothes that she had been able to survive, and she had come out of the hospital on Saturday none the worse for her adventure. Ram's cuts were healing, and he and his parents had come for a meal, and Dad had been quite nice to them and had driven them all to the Immigrant Center where they were to stay until the city renovated their front room. Fortunately the actual fire had gone no farther. The sofa had smoldered for a long time before catching fire.

Francis had even been praised and thanked for fetching the ladder, which he did not deserve in the least, and he felt closer to his mother than he had for a long time. Since that night in the kitchen he had really tried to be helpful and had almost decided to write Tyke a note saying he was not allowed out after dark anymore, when something happened to upset everything again.

It was a cold, wet Saturday morning, and Mum had persuaded Dad to take her shopping, and Francis and the girls had spent a fairly peaceful morning indoors, playing and watching television. Wendy and Debby cleaned out their dolls' house, and Francis was drawing. He had a whole folder of drawings, done mostly with felt tips, of football games, armies, planes, and dinosaurs, but he had never shown them to anyone. He suddenly thought his mother might like to see them, and he decided to spread them all out on the kitchen table, like an art exhibition, and show them to her when she came in.

But his parents were very late, and when they walked in the back door, it was clear that Dad was in a raging temper and Mum was crying. Dad took one look at the kitchen table.

"What on earth is all that trash doing on the table?" he barked. "Let's have some lunch. You could have set the table, couldn't you, Francis, instead of making all that mess?"

Francis went very red and dug in his heels. "It isn't trash," he said obstinately. "It's my pictures. I put 'em there to show 'em to Mum."

He turned eagerly to his mother, but she was not looking. "Just do what your dad tells you," she said wearily. "Must you start arguing the moment we get into the house?" She went up to her room and slammed the door, and they had to have lunch without her, Dad muttering angrily all the time, Wendy frightened, sulky, and inclined to pinch, and Debby crying for Mummy. There was really nothing to do but to join the gang again.

It was not at all difficult to slip out on Sunday, and
nothing much happened. They sat in the cold, dreary
little shed, telling jokes that Francis did not entirely
understand, and drank from a black bottle. But they
would not give Francis any. "It would go to your
head, see," said Tyke, "and you'd spit everything out.
Besides, you'd stink."

Not till after sunset, when the light had been lit, did
the real quiet fun begin. Sharp knives were passed
round, and Francis was told to run to the end of the
street again. There was a car parked halfway up.

"But you're not going to bash up the phone booth,
are you?" asked Francis anxiously. "They've fixed
it again."

"No, no, no, nothing like that," soothed Tyke, and
Spotty laughed gleefully. "I told you, just a little bit
of fun. You do what you're told, and we'll give you
a knife next time and let you run with us. Bonkers
can stand on guard."

Francis reached his sentry post and peeped to right
and left, but all was quiet. He stepped under the lamp
and waved, and the three boys set off as though running a race. Only when they reached the car did they
pause, lift their knives and systematically pierce each
tire. Then they sped on to separate at the T-junction.

But a fast car was approaching. It swerved around
the corner and jammed on its brakes to avoid hitting
the three flying figures. They stood for a second,
caught in the headlights, Bonkers still waving his
knife. Then they took to their heels, leaving Francis
paralyzed under the street lamp, unable to move for
fear. It had never occurred to him that his stepfather
might have a standing appointment with the fat, yellow-haired lady every Sunday night at seven thirty,

but unfortunately, that was the case. He was out of the car in a second and seized Francis by the wrists almost as roughly as Tyke had done.

"So this is what you're up to," he said, pushing Francis into the car. "That boy had a knife. You tell me instantly what you are all doing."

"Nuffing," sniffed Francis. "I was just standing there and they ran past."

"Rot!" said his stepfather. "Your sort doesn't just stand there in the dark for nothing. Either you tell me or I shall report what I've seen to the police. They'll make you talk fast enough. There was a phone booth wrecked here last week, and some windows broken in the next street. I suppose you know all about that too."

But Francis, remembering Tyke's threats, said nothing, and they sat in silence for some minutes, not far from the yellow-haired lady's house. Then a door opened farther down the street. A man came out and jumped into the parked car. He pressed on his accelerator, and there was a strange, dragging sound. He stopped, got out, and examined his tires. Then he walked deliberately towards Dad's car.

"All four tires punctured," he said heavily. "You didn't happen to see anyone, did you? I wasn't long in the house, and they were all right when I arrived."

"I nearly knocked over three boys," said Dad, "and I believe this young stepson of mine knows something about it. One of 'em had a knife, and I'm going to get the police onto this because you aren't the first. Just give me your name and address. There's a garage just around the corner. I'm sorry about your tires."

Dad was getting impatient and was probably anxious about keeping the yellow-haired girl waiting. He

suddenly turned the car and drove back home at high
speed. He pulled Francis out and pushed him into the
kitchen.

"Out with some gang, slashing tires," he shouted at
his startled wife. "I'm going to get the police onto it
tomorrow—I'm fed up with the whole business. Can't
you even look after your own kid?"

He was gone, roaring down the street again, and his
mother sent Francis upstairs because she did not know
what else to do. But later, when the girls were in bed,
she came up and knelt down beside him.

"Francis, tell me what you've been doing!"

He longed to fling his arms around her neck and tell
her everything, but he was too afraid of Tyke. Tyke
was going to jump out from behind some bushes and
beat him up if he told.

"I didn't do nothing, honest, Mum. I just stood at
the corner of the street, and they ran past me."

"Who's 'they'?"

"I dunno. Three boys."

"But what street, Francis?"

"The street where Ram lives. Dad came round the
corner again."

"The same street where you saw him last time?"

"Yep."

"The same house?"

"I dunno. He saw me and stopped."

"No one came out?"

"No. Mum, I didn't do nothing wrong. I'm awfully hungry. Couldn't I have some supper?"

She went away and came back with a supper tray.
He sat up and ate a hearty meal, while she sat beside
him, worrying. There was no doubt that he had
turned into a shocking little liar, and she did not know

whether to believe him or not.

A policewoman called next day, but she could not get anything out of him either. She asked him a lot of questions, while his dad sat listening, but he had a vague feeling that she liked him better than she did his stepfather.

"I was just standing, and they ran past me," he kept repeating quite calmly. He was far more afraid of Tyke than he was of the policewoman.

"But what were you doing, just standing?" she asked.

"Just going for a little walk."

"Where to?"

"Nowhere. Just playing round. They suddenly ran past me."

"Where from?"

Francis hesitated and knew that she was watching him very carefully indeed.

"Up the road."

"From the end of the road?"

"Yep—I think so. I dunno."

The policewoman made a little note on her pad.

"What did they look like?"

"Big. One had a big black beard."

"That's a lie," said his stepfather. "They were just a pack of kids, not more than fourteen or fifteen at the most."

Francis fell silent. He had quite forgotten that his stepfather had seen them too.

"Well," said the policewoman at last, turning away from Francis, "there's nothing to prove that he was involved. He may be speaking the truth or he may not. But it's up to you, Mr. West. Know what he's doing all the time and keep him in after dark for his own sake as well as for other people's. There's a very rough gang about, and we're on their tracks. Just see to it that he doesn't get mixed up with them. He's only ten; you should be able to control him."

"That's his mother's job," replied Dad angrily, and he repeated all that the policewoman had said to his wife, with a little more added on. She listened, deeply troubled, knowing that while she grieved and pined over her husband, unable to give her mind to anything else, something was going very wrong indeed with her young son.

8

Flight

For the next three days things went from bad to worse at home. The fat yellow-haired girl became a recognized person whom Mum and Dad quarreled about, and she had a name: Gloria. Dad came home late and appeared only at breakfast. Mum went about looking like a ghost, with dark circles under her eyes, and did not seem able to listen to what anyone said. She was always lying down with headaches or crying, and Wendy and Debby did exactly what they liked. In Francis's view, they became more and more cheeky. Outside, the spring surged to its fulfillment, and the yards were gay with daffodils, tulips, and blossoms, but inside the house seemed to get colder and drearier every day.

And then came a terrible morning when Mum did not come down to breakfast at all, and Dad gave them their meal and seemed to want to hustle them all off to school in a great hurry. He always dropped off Wendy and Debby on his way to work, but Francis went on the bus and saw no reason to start just after eight.

"It isn't time," he argued. "I shall get there too early. Besides, I haven't said good-bye to Mum."

"Well, you can't say good-bye to her today. She's

not well enough. I want you out of the house before I leave, see?"

"Why? And anyhow, it's too early for Wendy and Deb. You needn't be at work till nine."

"Look here, Francis, *will* you stop arguing and go! I'm not going to work today. I'm coming back to take Mum to the doctor. She's very unwell, so don't make things more difficult than they are. You're holding up everything as usual, so get out!"

He got out in a hurry because he did not want Dad to see his tears welling up and overflowing. It was all Dad's fault, he thought, that Mum was ill; it all had something vaguely to do with Gloria. He was wretched and inattentive at school and got a bad conduct mark, but he did not care. He wanted to go home, but when he rushed into the house at four o'clock there were old Mrs. Glengarry washing dishes at the sink and Wendy and Debby, quiet and well-behaved, cutting out paper dolls' clothes at the kitchen table.

"Where's Mum?" said Francis abruptly.

"I'm afraid your mum's not well and has to stay in the hospital for a time, dear," said Mrs. Glengarry kindly. "I just came over to give you your tea, till your Dad comes at six. Now you've come, we'll put the kettle on, and Wendy will show me where everything is and help set the table."

"Me too," said Debby, who usually never wanted to help.

The girls were all graciousness and helpfulness, and tea passed pleasantly. Mrs. Glengarry had made them a cake and told them comfortable stories about her cats that made Wendy and Debby laugh. But Francis felt desolate. Halfway through tea he pushed back his plate and said loudly, "Mrs. Glengarry, how long will Mum have to stay in the hospital? And when can I go and see her? Could I go on the bus now? I know the way."

Mrs. Glengarry hesitated. "I'm afraid she's not in that hospital, dear," she said. "She's gone to a special hospital farther out, and she's not allowed visitors at present. But you could write her a letter. Would that help?"

"Not really," said Francis. "I'm not very good at writing letters. Mrs. Glengarry, what's the matter with my mum?"

The old lady looked troubled.

"I think you'll have to ask your dad about that, Francis," she said quietly. "I'm sure he'll explain. You've noticed your mother hasn't been too well lately, haven't you? I think it's all the same thing. It's not a dangerous illness; she just needs rest."

"She had headaches and she cried," said Francis, "but she wasn't ill. May I leave the table, please?" Tears were welling up again, and he ran out into the yard and sought refuge in the cherry tree. It was just bursting into blossom, like a great white tent, and he had once imagined that he would sit here with Mum. Whatever would happen to them all without Mum? Perhaps Granny would come. He liked Granny, but she did not get along with Dad, and she would not be at all pleased about Gloria.

It would soon be sunset. He watched a thrush fly home to its nest in the hedge, and the sky, through the gaps in the young blossoms, glowed brightly, tinging the white petals with pink. It was so quiet, and Mum could have rested here. Then he saw Mrs. Glengarry go home to feed her cats, and he thought he had better

get back to Wendy and Deb. There would be an awful
row if he was not there when Dad came home.

Mrs. Glengarry had left everything in perfect order,
and the little girls seemed unusually peaceful. When
Dad came in they were all playing happily, and he
switched on the television and sat down beside them.

"What's the matter with Mum?" asked Francis.
"Why can't I go and see her?"

"Because she has gone to a hospital out in the
country, and she will have to stay there for a time.
She'll be all right, Francis. It's her nerves, and she
just needs a good rest."

"How long will she stay there?"

"I really don't know, but don't worry. We're going to fix things up tomorrow. In the meantime, there's
supper to think about, isn't there? How about going
to the fish-and-chip shop, Francis, and bringing us all
a nice hot supper?"

The little girls clapped their hands. They loved
fish and chips.

Francis took the money and set off along the dark
street. He walked slowly because he hated being at
home without Mum, even with fish and chips. He was
glad there was a line and he would have to wait, but
he was not glad to see Spotty ahead of him. He turned
his head as Spotty left the shop and hoped he had
got rid of him, but when he finally made his pur-
chase and stepped out into the street, there was Spotty
waiting.

"I'm walkin' home with you," said Spotty mysteri-
ously. "How come you told the police about our hideout?"

"I didn't," said Francis, startled. "I never told
them nothing. Honest, I didn't. She asked me ques-

tions and I just said—"

"Oh, yes, we know all about her," said Spotty, who had known nothing about her till that moment. "And if you never told her nothing, how come they found the hideout and boarded it all up? Not that it bothers us—we'll find another, but we shan't tell you. I always said you were soft. Tyke's going to do you in for this."

He seized Francis's package, flung it on the ground, and kicked him on the shins. Francis flew at him and punched him in the stomach. Spotty grabbed his hair, hit him in the face, and then sent him sprawling on the ground, after which he took to his heels. He did not really like fighting; it made him too breathless.

Francis got up slowly. His lip was cut and bleeding and his hands covered with mud, but, worst of all, the fish and chips had fallen out on the pavement. The fish was all in pieces, and however hard he tried to scrape the dirt off the chips, he could not remove it all. He wrapped them up again and crept home feeling sore and frightened. His father was in the kitchen setting the table.

"You've taken your time, haven't you, Francis?" he snapped. "And—good night, what have you been doing? You look as though you have been fighting."

"I fell down, Dad. I'm sorry. I'm afraid I fell on top of the fish and chips and it got a bit squashed."

He handed the sad-looking package to his father, who stared at it in disgust. "Well," he said at last, "it's your supper, so you'll have to make the best of it. But you're a clumsy one, aren't you! Can't even go to the fish shop without messing everything up. Now call the girls and come and eat."

Nothing went well. Wendy made loud and un-

necessary remarks about the grit in her chips, and
when it was bedtime, Debby started crying for Mum.
Dad, who had tried hard to begin with, grew short-
tempered, and Francis watched a program that did
not interest him and then wandered up to bed. His
lip hurt, he was miserable about his mother, and ter-
rified of Tyke. Tyke could beat him up as easy as
winking.

He wondered what would happen if he went down
now in his pajamas, told Dad all about it, and asked
him to protect him. His dad did not like him much,
but there were moments when he had been kind.
Once he had bought him a bicycle, twice he had taken
him to a football game, and he had often bought him
ice cream and taken him swimming. When Wendy
was still little and had not started pinching, they had
been quite good friends. And anyhow, even if he was
very angry, his stepfather would not let him be beaten.

With a pounding heart he jumped out of bed and
hurried downstairs on bare feet. Dad would be watching television in the living room. He crouched at the
door listening. But the set was switched off, and Dad
was talking and laughing in a way that he never did
with Mum. And someone was talking back in an excited, giggly voice.

I suppose Gloria's come to visit him, thought Francis. *I'll have to wait. I'll leave the bedroom door
open, and then I'll hear when she goes.*

But he never heard her go for he fell asleep, and
next morning they all went off to school in a hurry,
and there was no chance to talk. Francis spent his
time out of class keeping well out of Tyke's way. He
jumped on the bus the minute school was over and
ran all the way from the bus stop. It was a warm,

sunny day, and the girls were playing in the yard.

"Dad's got a visitor," said Wendy. "We can't have tea till he goes."

"Do you mean *she?*" asked Francis rather drearily. This was getting to be too much of a good thing.

"No, it's a he. Dad called him Dr. somebody. They're in the living room. You've got to wait."

Francis walked very quietly into the house and put down his school bag. The living room door was not quite shut, and he stood irresolute in the hall. He could hear most of what they said, and if this was a doctor, then he wanted to hear.

"I believe there's some talk of a divorce, isn't there, Mr. West?" said an even voice. "Could this be the real root of your wife's trouble?"

"Oh, I don't know about that," answered Dad, sounding rather put out. "But we can't go on like this. Unfortunately, things just aren't working out between me and my wife—"

"I see. Well, she'll have to be under care for some time. She's in the throes of a very bad nervous break-down, and what is troubling her at the moment is, What is going to happen to the children? I presume you can't keep on your job and look after them?"

"Not really," said Dad, "but I've been thinking it out, and I had a talk with the manager this morning. He was most helpful. The little girls can go to my mother, and I have asked for a transfer. Our business has a plant up north not too far from where my mother lives, and there's a vacancy next week. I shall have to shut up the house for a time and get an apartment near my job."

"And what about the boy? Will he go too?"

"I'm afraid not. He's not my boy, and he's a bit

of a problem at the moment, getting into bad company and that sort of thing. My mother couldn't possibly be responsible, and besides, she hasn't room for three children. He will have to go into a foster home."

"That seems rather rough on the little chap. Isn't there another granny who could have him?"

"My wife's mother lives in a one-room apartment and has arthritis. She'll come down to be near my wife, but she couldn't cope with the house and the boy. I think she'll stay with friends."

"I see. Then it's just a matter of getting in touch with the Social Services and finding some place for the boy."

Francis had stood rooted to the spot, but he suddenly realized that the conversation was coming to a close, and whatever happened he must not be found in the hall. Besides he would have to act very fast indeed. He knew about going into foster homes; he had a friend in one. Tyke would almost certainly beat him up if he was in a foster home, as it would not be like having his own folks to protect him.

And suddenly he knew where he was going. He got his bicycle and pedaled very fast down the path and into the road. "Tell Dad I've gone for a ride," he shouted to Wendy. "I don't want any tea."

He was off, with the sweet spring wind blowing his hair backward, down the main road and off to the right. Now he was in the country, and the birds were singing. There were tufts of emerald on the hawthorn hedges, and the banks were starred with celandines and primroses, but apart from a general sense of greenness and hopefulness he did not notice much.

He was trying to decide what he was going to say. He could not help knowing that he had made rather a poor impression on his first visit, and this time he must do better. There was always plenty to do on a farm, and he would milk cows, feed pigs—anything. He was rather hazy about farms, but he would convince them that he was a wonderful worker, and the Easter holidays were just about to start. If only he could keep out of Tyke's clutches till then, he would be safe. Tyke would never find him there.

He was coasting through the village, thinking of more and more things that he could do, and by the time he reached the bridge over the river he had come to think that they were very lucky to get him. The water had gone down considerably since the day of his great adventure. He could see the road that led right to the farm.

It was still broad daylight, and he stood for a time at the gate, considering exactly how to introduce himself. "I've come to help you with the cows"? But the cows, lying peacefully in the daisies, did not look as though they needed any help at all. "You'll need some weeding done, now that spring's come"? or, "I thought you might like an extra boy on the farm"? Any of those might do. He would decide when he got there.

He stuck out his chest, marched up the path, and knocked loudly on the door.

The farmer opened it and found himself looking down into the face of a small boy with a swollen lip and very bright, anxious, brown eyes, who seemed vaguely familiar.

And Francis, looking up at the large, friendly figure of the farmer, suddenly forgot all his fine speeches. His eyes filled with tears again.

"I've got to go into a foster home," he blurted out. "I just wondered—do you think you could possibly care for me?"

9

Refuge

"Come right in," said the farmer. "Aren't you the little chap who took our boat?"

It seemed a bad beginning. Francis sniffed sadly and stepped inside. The family was having a noisy tea in the kitchen, but the farmer led Francis into a little sort of office, and they both sat down.

"Do your parents know you've come?" asked the farmer.

"Mum's in the hospital," replied Francis. "Dad knows I've gone for a bike ride. I've got to go into a foster home.

"So you said before," said the farmer. "Have you had some tea?"

Francis shook his head. The farmer went away and came back with a mug of tea and a slice of homemade cake. When it was finished, the farmer leaned back in his chair. "Now tell me all about it," he said.

And Francis, warmed and fortified by tea and cake, and encouraged by the deeply attentive man in front of him, went on. With the help of a few questions, he told everything, and by the time he had finished, the farmer knew all about Tyke, Spotty, the telephone booth, Ram, the fire, Mum, Dad, Wendy, Debby, and the police. It was quite a story, and when he had finished, Francis looked up pleadingly.

"So, you see," he said, "If you can't care for me, I don't know where I shall go, and Tyke will get me. But you'd have to care for my cat too, 'cause she can't go to Yorkshire, and she can't stay alone, so she'd have to come, wouldn't she?"

"Of course," agreed the farmer. "If you come, the cat comes too. She could be the official barn mouser."

Francis laughed gaily and had a queer feeling that it was the first time he had laughed like that for quite a while.

"I'm going to phone your father and talk to my wife," said the farmer. He was gone for about twenty minutes while Francis thumbed through pamphlets about the milk board. When he came back he was smiling.

"Come on," he said. "You can leave your bike in the shed. I'm taking you home to have a chat with your dad."

They drove in silence for both had quite a lot to think about, and when they arrived, Mr. West came to the door to meet them, looking rather uncomfortable.

"Good evening," he said. "I'm sorry to have put you to all this trouble. I had no idea where Francis had gone. Francis, go and eat your supper. Come in here, Mr. Glenny."

They talked for quite a time. Then Dad put his head around the kitchen door and said, "All right, Francis, they very kindly say they'll have you, and Mr. Glenny will take you now. There's an empty suitcase in our bedroom. Run upstairs and collect what you need."

Francis shot upstairs and shoved his clothes into the suitcase. He was just about to start on his toy cupboard when his stepfather appeared. "Come along," he said. "You'll only need your clothes. You can't take all that junk. The gentleman's waiting. You've got some nerve, haven't you! However, it seems to be turning out for the best. Now, step on it!"

"I want my toys," protested Francis, "and my stamps and my football cards. I can't go without them."

"You'll do what you're told," said Dad, slamming down the lid of the suitcase and giving him a shove. "There'll be plenty of toys where he comes from." He hurried Francis downstairs to where Mr. Glenny stood waiting in the front hall. Francis stuck his head around the kitchen door.

" 'Bye, Wendy, 'bye, Debby," he shouted. "I'm going away, and I'm not coming back till Mum's better."

And then a terrible thing happened. Wendy, who had been absorbed in a jigsaw puzzle, looked up and suddenly understood. She ran to him, flung her arms round his middle, and burst into tears. "Francis, Francis," she sobbed, "don't go. Dad'll go out at night, and we shall be alone in the house. Oh, Francie, stay!"

Francis was too surprised to speak for a moment. He had always thought that he and Wendy hated each other, but now he was not so sure. She gazed tragically up at him, and he saw, for the first time in his life, how soft and pretty her hair was and how blue her eyes. He put his arm around her.

"You'll be all right," he said gruffly. "You're going to Gran in Yorkshire. You're lucky, you are."

He quite forgot that he was not meant to know. Wendy's eyes sparkled through her tears. "To Gran

in Yorkshire?" she repeated joyously, and Debby
said, "Gran in Yorkser gave me a teddy bear. 'Bye,
Francis."

"Mum'll soon be better, and we'll all come back,"
he whispered to Wendy and gave her an awkward little kiss on the top of her head. Then he seized his
suitcase, and everyone searched for the cat, who had
disappeared. Francis found her under the bed and
hurried to the car without a backward look. He stuck
his head out the window and breathed in the warm
spring night. As last he felt safe.

Everyone welcomed him and seemed glad to see
him when they arrived. Kate was doing her home-
work at the table, and Martin and Chris sat by the
fire in their robes, playing battleships. Mrs. Glenny
took his suitcase. "We'll show you your room when
we've all had a cup of tea," she said cheerfully. "It's
a little one all of your own, under the roof. John,
dear, we've finished outside, and we waited for
prayers till you came."

I wonder what 'prayers' means, thought Francis.
It sounds like school.

They gathered around the fire in a warm circle with
their cups of tea, and little Chris climbed onto his
mother's lap. Their father picked up a Bible and
turned the pages. "Only sixteen days till Easter," he
said, "so we'll go on reading what Jesus said to his
disciples the night before He died, in John 13."

They were halfway through some story Francis
did not know, so he did not listen. Instead, he found
himself staring at that funny card on the wall and wondering what it meant. God Is Luv. Then he was suddenly arrested by the last words that Mr. Glenny was
reading. " 'A new commandment I give to you, that

you love one another, even as I have loved you, that you also love one another. By this all men will know that you are My disciples, if you have love for one another.' "

You did not seem able to get away from love in this house, however you liked to spell it. It drew him, and he wanted to think about it. Nobody had loved much at home. Mum and Dad quarreled, Wendy pinched, and when he tried to love Mum, she usually did not listen or seem to notice. Tyke and Spotty hated all the time. Being with them had been fun at first, but looking back now, it all seemed rather cold and sad and frightening. If they had loved, perhaps Mum would not have had headaches and gone to the hospital, and he would not feel so afraid of going back to school. Perhaps, he thought vaguely, loving was a better, happier way. But how did you start?

He thought about it again when he was lying in bed in his little attic, listening to the owls hooting and watching the stars through the skylight. Mrs. Glenny had helped him unpack, tucked him in, and kissed him good-night. Whiskers lay curled up on the quilt beside him because it was too late to take her to the barn that night. He felt cozy, sleepy, and safe. He remembered the night he had sat with Mum in the kitchen after the fire—and how Whiskers had purred on his chest after he had kicked her—faithful little Ram bringing him presents—Wendy flinging her arms round his middle. There was quite a lot of love about if you really looked for it. God Is Luv. He had better find out about God. They could do with a bit more love where he came from.

10

Questions

Francis went to church with the family for the first time on Sunday and thought that he might find out something about God there. But he could make nothing of the service, and halfway through he decided that he had better give up. So he spent the sermon time drumming his heels and thinking about Tyke.

But even if he could not understand in church, there was no mistaking the love at home. It took Francis only a short while to discover that where a mother and father truly love each other, children are happy and busy and no one wants to pinch or quarrel much. There was a lot of laughter too and pleasure in being together.

The time they all seemed closest was when they sat on the hearthrug after supper and Mr. Glenny read the Bible to them and prayed. Each night of that week they read more of what Jesus said to His disciples the night before He died, and it seemed to Francis that they must all have stayed up very late to have heard as much as that. He did not understand a great deal except that word *love,* which came over and over again. Jesus seemed to think it was extremely important.

He was rather disappointed about helping on the

farm. This farm was quite unlike his toy model or farms he had read about in books, and Uncle John's great concern was that he should keep out of the way of the machinery.

However, there were moments! He liked going out in the evening to call in the cattle and then running ahead to stand on the platform in the stall and watch them come in orderly procession to munch their feed. He liked the hum of the machinery and the sound of the swirling milk cascading into the great refrigerated container. Even more, he enjoyed carrying the food to the calves and watching them jostle each other on wobbly legs, plunging their noses into the mixture, or, as they grew older, butting their foreheads together as they fought for their feed. Uncle John had a herd of forty pedigreed Friesans, and a number of them were calving just then. One never-to-be forgotten night they all crouched quietly on the straw in their robes and watched a calf being born.

But what he really loved best was the river. Whenever he could, he would escape and run along the banks, watching the swans, the ducks, and the moorhens, and sometimes throwing stones at them for fun. He found the dam and noticed that, after a rather dry March, the water looked quite shallow. He wondered how they had ever felt so frightened. He wandered farther, to the place where the tributary joined the larger river and found fan-shaped beaches where the cattle came down to drink in the early morning. One day he and Martin painted the little boat, brought down the oars, and went for a ride in it. But the ride was not as exciting as before because it kept sticking in the reeds.

He liked Martin, but privately thought him a rather

tame little boy, perfectly content with his home, his school, his village Scout pack, and the countryside. Francis felt he could teach him a thing or two, and tried one day when they were sauntering down the riverbank, looking for swans' nests in the reeds. The lambs in the pastures on the other side were making a tremendous crying, and Martin was telling him about some boys who had tried to steal a swan's egg, and the police had gone after them because swans belong to the Queen and are under royal protection.

"Pooh!" said Francis. "That's nothing. Before I came here, I belonged to a gang that had knives and bombs and things. The police caught me, but I didn't tell 'em a thing. It's easy to fool the police."

"But what did you do with guns and bombs?" asked Martin.

"Oh, we—we slashed tires and bashed up phone booths, and—blew people up."

"Why? Whatever for?"

Francis hesitated. He had no answer to that one. Why had they done it?

"Oh, just for fun!" he answered rather lamely.

"Well, it doesn't sound much fun to me, and I bet it wasn't much fun for the people who got blown up. Besides, I don't believe it. Children don't have bombs. Look at those two long-tailed tits—I think they're going to build a nest. Stand still, and watch."

Francis scowled at Martin, standing motionless among the celandines and daisies, far more interested in two silly little birds than in his own dangerous and glorious deeds. And he was not any more successful with little Chris. He and Chris were sitting on the step together eating bread and jam, and Chris was jigging excitedly up and down.

"I'm going to Cubs tonight in my new uniform," he announced. "Are you going to Scouts, Francis?"

"No!" scoffed Francis, who wanted to go very much. "You do sissy things in Scouts. I belonged to a real gang before I came here, and we used to go out at night with guns and knives and things."

Chris looked at him, neither shocked nor impressed, merely entertained.

"What did you do with them?" he asked. "Did you kill people dead?"

Francis, glancing round to see that Auntie Alison was well out of earshot, started off on a highly colored account of his own evil deeds. Chris listened calmly enough.

"Well," he said at last, "you're not as clever as my daddy. We had a cow what nearly died, and my daddy made it come alive again. It's much cleverer to make something alive what was dead than to make something dead what was alive, so there!"

Francis gave up. "What do you know?" he muttered. "You and your old Scouts!"

He stumped upstairs and lay down on his bed with his dirty boots on, because he was not allowed to, and stayed there sulking for a time. He felt homesick for his mother, even homesick for the gang, and yet those questions nagged at him. Why had they done it? Had it really been fun? Was healing and helping really better than bashing and destroying? Was loving better than hating and pinching? He had only been at the farm for ten days, and yet he was having so many strange new thoughts. It was all most bewildering.

Later on, he sat alone at the kitchen table, bored and cross, turning the pages of a magazine. Uncle John was out milking, Kate was monopolizing the television with a program that did not interest him, and Auntie Alison was ironing. Martin and Chris had gone off to Scouts and Cubs and had invited him to go too, but, after all he had said, he was too proud to accept. He would make some excuse and go the following week. In the meantime—his gaze wandered around the room and came back, as usual, to rest on the misspelled card on the wall.

"Auntie Alison," he said suddenly, "Where's God?"

Auntie Alison nearly dropped the iron. She had quite forgotten the cross boy at the table.

"God?" she repeated. "He's—He's everywhere." She paused to think. "Everything you see, Francis— the flowers, the river, the calves, the birds, the stars— all life and color and beauty come from Him. God is like the source of a beautiful river."

"Yes, but where is He?" persisted Francis.

She switched off the iron and came and sat down beside him. "It's a good question, Francis," she said, "because you'll never be happy until you find Him. All love and happiness flow from Him, and He wants you to find Him. He loves you—He came to you—"

"*What?*" said Francis.

"Yes, He came to you in Jesus. We couldn't see God, so He became a Man. Jesus said, 'If you have seen Me, you have seen My Father, God.' Listen very carefully when we read about Jesus at night, because when you begin to know Jesus, you'll begin to know God. God showed us His love in Jesus—Jesus spent His whole life loving, healing, and helping, and in the end He died because He loved us so much— you'll hear about that tomorrow night because it is the evening before Good Friday, the day Jesus died on the cross about two thousand years ago. People still remember that day all over the world."

She was speaking very slowly, uncertain how best to explain, and Francis stared out the window at the last light behind the line of poplars along the riverbank. This conversation had started up a new train of thought.

"All rivers have sources, don't they?" he said.

"Yes."

"Where's the source of this river?"

"I don't know, but I could find out. Somewhere, far up in the hills, there must be a spring, bubbling up from the earth, and the rainfall's high up there, so it gets bigger and bigger and other streams join it, and wherever they go, everything grows green and beautiful."

Francis was silent. Much of what Auntie Alison had said had gone over his head, but two things remained, because anything to do with the river fascinated him. "God is like the source of a beautiful river—all love and happiness flow from Him."

Kate came in at that point, put on the light, and offered to get supper. Kate was fifteen, tall and slender with long, fair hair. She did not approve of Francis and thought her parents were far too lenient with him, and Francis considered her a perfect pain. He was not going to talk in front of her, so he stepped out into the dusk that smelled so sweet of new grass, catkin pollen, and cows, and wandered down to the river.

It lapped in the reeds where the swans and moorhens were going to nest. A water rat splashed in the amber current and made him jump. "God is like the source of a beautiful river—all love and happiness flow from Him." If he could somehow find that source, he supposed he would be happy. And perhaps

Mum and Dad would love each other, and Gloria would get out—and Mum would get better—and Wendy would stop pinching, and Tyke would stop wanting to do him in.

What else had she said? He tried to remember. "When you begin to know Jesus, you'll begin to know God." He had better listen very carefully tonight.

11

The Source

Francis listened every night and, because it seemed like an interesting story, he learned a lot. He learned how Jesus died on Good Friday because He loved people and wanted to take the punishment of their wrong-doing on Himself. He also learned that Jesus rose again on Easter day, was alive now, and still went on loving. Then they started reading stories about His life on earth—healing, helping, loving. It was love, love, love all the time.

That was all very nice, but it made no difference to Francis. He still threw stones at the ducks and did all he dared to annoy Kate. When no one was looking, he still snatched nice food to take to the river, and he told stories that were not true. Mum was getting better, so they said, so he supposed they would soon be going home. He wanted to see Mum, but he did not want to go home, because once they got home the whole business would start over again. Dad and Gloria would reappear, Wendy would start pinching, and Tyke would be near enough to do him in. There seemed no end to it, because there was no new beginning.

The Easter holidays seemed to fly, because there was so much to do. He, Martin, and Chris helped on the farm and messed about with the boat. They made a house on an island, swam, fished, and looked for nests. Francis enjoyed it all, but he was happiest when he was by, on, or in the river. He could not have explained why he loved the river so much. Perhaps it was because his first great adventure had had to do with the river, or perhaps because it had washed him up at the feet of Uncle John. He was obsessed with its course and would trace it out on the map or lie in bed imagining it flowing on and on, broadening, to the great cities and the sea. Sometimes in thought he would trace it backwards to the spring, high up in the hills, where the first silver trickle bubbled over and swelled to a current. When he grew up, that was the first thing he would do—he would follow the river right back to its source.

There were only three days left of the Easter holidays. Kate was rejoicing, and Martin was grumbling at having to go back to school. After prayers that night, Uncle John made an announcement.

"There's a lot that needs to be done in the yard tomorrow," he said. "The lawn needs mowing, the flower beds weeding, and the compost dug in for the next plantings. If we all worked hard tomorrow, we could get that done, and the next day we will have a holiday. Martin, Francis, and Chris, I'll take you all to the cattle market, and Mum can have a quiet day at home. You can come too, if you want, Kate."

"I'll help tomorrow and stay home and finish my essay on Wednesday," said Kate, who was very studious.

"Then you'll have the house to yourself," said her mother. "I'm going to the hairdresser's."

"Good!" replied Kate. "I like the house to myself.

It's nice and quiet." She glanced meaningfully at Francis, who was in the habit of playing "Chopsticks" on the piano. They had never actually had a quarrel, for to Francis, Kate was almost grown-up, but she had said several things to him that he did not intend to forget. One day Kate was going to get what was coming. He went upstairs to bed muttering rather viciously, and it struck him that he was not really looking forward to spending the best part of tomorrow working, with Kate watching him out of the corner of her eye, ready to pounce on him if he slacked. It was not his idea of fun at all. He was not a servant, and he was not going to do anything he did not like doing. Perhaps he would do something else.

He fell asleep hating Kate, but as he slept he had a wonderful dream. He dreamed that he was running along the bank of the river toward the source, but the riverbed was dry, and the banks were caked mud like the desert in the geography book. Then he saw a stream trickling from the hills, and wherever the water came, life, beauty, greenness, and buttercups sprang up. *A river of life,* he said to himself and woke to find the sun streaming through his window and the first cuckoo calling outside. *A river of life,* he repeated and wondered where he had heard those words before. He rather thought that it must have been in church.

He sprang out of bed in a great hurry, feeling the kiss of the sun on his bare skin. He did not really mean to be naughty. It was his dream that had put the idea into his head. There would not be many days before he went back to school, and he must have a day to himself to do his own thing. Uncle John always got up early but not quite so early as this, and he thought he could just make it. He stuffed some biscuits and cold meat into his pocket and on the table left a note that said, "I'm gone. I will come back. Love, Francis."

He brought his bicycle from the garage and gave a great sigh of relief as the trees screened him from view. He was going to follow the river, keeping close to the banks, and although he knew that he could not possibly reach the source in the hills, he would go as far as he could. There were other little green, wooded hills on the horizon.

He started off along the road, pedaling between hedges, but he soon discovered that it was impossible to follow the road and stick to the river; he kept losing it. So when he reached the nearest village he asked a friendly garage man if he might leave his bicycle there as he wanted to go for a walk. The man was most agreeable. He pointed out the path that led to the river and gave Francis a bag of chips. So he trotted off through the buttercups, and the sense of freedom, the sunshine, the birdsong, the kindness, and the chips cast a sort of heavenly glow over that April morning that Francis never forgot for the rest of his life.

Even on foot, it was not always easy to follow the river. Sometimes there was a path, and sometimes he had to push through hedges or squeeze through barbed wire or skirt fields of young green wheat. He trotted several miles, and the morning shadows had shortened, and the day was getting hotter. But the river did not appear to be growing any smaller.

Every step was interesting. He came to a wood, dim and scented with bluebells. Here he sat down and ate his lunch, watching the sun-flecked water through feathery beech leaves. A little later he saw a kingfisher dart out of a hole and skim the surface of the river. The banks smelled of garlic, and in one field a family of rabbits were washing their ears. And he never, for a moment, felt lonely. The chatter and gurgle of the river and the crying of sheep and lambs were company enough for anyone. He lost all count of time and could have wandered on forever, happily planning how to annoy Kate, or just thinking about the river.

"The river of life," he murmured to himself. "The source of a beautiful river."

It was midafternoon and very hot when the ground on either side of him began to rise, and he realized that he had reached the hilly country. *"Far, far away in some high hills!"* Perhaps he had gotten there. The river did seem a little narrower, and he did not know that it was a good deal deeper.

And then, as he rounded a shoulder of the meadow, he found it—a clear stream rushing down over golden stones to join the river. Forget-me-nots and shining buttercups grew on the banks and in the marshy patches at the side, for it had tunneled itself a little valley. Francis, gazing upwards, thought that if he followed it away up into those hills, he might find the source. He strung his sandals around his neck with a bit of string and began climbing, following the stream.

It was not always easy because the hillside was very steep, and the stream cascaded down in merry little waterfalls. Sometimes he had to pull himself up by bundles of fern and grass, and sometimes the land flattened out into daisy-starred pastureland. The river was below him now, a sparkling ribbon winding between weeping willows and alders until it disap-

peared behind another fold of the hills. He would
have to wait till he grew up to track that river to its
source, but this one was within his grasp. He just
had to climb to the top.

He was nearly there. He had now reached a sloping
field that seemed to him greener than any field he had
ever seen before. All over it skipped lambs, and sheep
lay grazing. It was nearly shearing time, and their
full fleeces seemed white as the fluffy clouds above the
hilltop. It would be easy going from here onwards,
because the stream laughed its way through a pasture
and led to a house that stood right on the crest,
sheltered by a thicket of larches.

"Perhaps the man who lives in that house looks
after the source," thought Francis, hurrying on, "but
I'm going to find it by myself first." It was not at all
difficult now that he had come so far. Just by the
house was a stone trough set in the ground full of
water. Just above it, near the roots of the trees, was
a shallow, bubbling well with a pipe where one could
fill buckets, and the water that bubbled up in the well
was spring water, clear as crystal. The ferns, forget-
me-nots, and periwinkles that grew all around it were
longer, greener, and bluer than any he had ever seen
before.

He sat on the little wall of the well, dangled his
bruised feet in the water, and looked around him.
The windswept larches leaned toward the south, their
crimson tufts jeweling the new green. Far below lay
the great plain with its wheat fields, farms, wooded
pastures, river valley, villages, and church spires.
Francis could see most of the way he had come, and
he thought it would not be too difficult to get home
again. He had no idea how late it was.

"Hey, you young varmint, what for you fouling up my spring with your dirty feet? Take 'em out, I say, before I set the dog on you."

Francis leaped up, and the angry shepherd, seeing how very small he was, spoke more gently.

"Now where be you come from?" he asked. "You don't be from these parts. And did no one ever teach you about fouling good spring water? Don't you let me catch you doing that again!"

"Sorry," said Francis, keeping his eye on the panting collie. "I didn't know. I followed the stream all the way up from the river, and I followed the river all the way from Rockleigh. Is this the real true source, and does it belong to you?"

"Rockleigh?" repeated the shepherd. "That's a long way for a little chap like you to come all alone."

Francis nodded. "Did you find this source," he said, "or did you dig for it? Did you see clear water bubbling out of the ground?"

The shepherd chuckled. He was beginning to like this wet, dirty little apparition. The spring was the pride of his life and had been the pride of his father's life.

"You'd best come inside," he said. "My woman'll tell you all about it. I'm busy. But what I'm thinking is, How do you figure out getting back to Rockleigh tonight?"

"I left a bike somewhere," said Francis vaguely. "In the next village along the road. It was called Upper Bowbridge. I just need to get back there."

He had followed the shepherd into a stone kitchen where a bright-eyed little woman had just made a pot of tea and a tame lamb lay on the hearthrug. Visitors were few on that lonely hilltop where her husband kept his sheep, and she seemed pleased to see Francis.

"Look at this, Mother," said the shepherd with a wink. "Found 'im fouling the spring with his dirty feet. He's followed the river from Rockleigh, and what I'm asking is, How's he getting back?—not more than a couple of hours till sunset."

"The mailman'll take him," said Mother calmly. "I'll run him down to the mailbox in half an hour. The truck goes right into Rockleigh. Sit down, sonny, and have a cup of tea."

He was very hungry indeed and started off on a package of buns with the best will in the world. The shepherd, gulping down his tea, made his farewells.

"Mother'll tell you about the spring," he said, "but remember this—sheep won't drink from fouled water—never you foul a spring. Well, I'll be getting to the sheep. So long, son."

Francis sat on the rug beside the tame lamb and asked questions. He learned that years ago the shepherd's father had climbed the hill in time of drought and found a winding patch of deep green grass at the edge of the wood. "So he knowed it was water deep down tunneling into the ground and a-watering the roots, so he dug down deep. The water was all fouled with mud and dead leaves and roots of trees, but he cleared it and dug the spring a little further down, and the water soon came up clear and clean. Then he built his house and bought his flock and brought up my mother-in-law. My hubby was born here on the hill, and I came here as a bride. There were brothers and sisters, but they've gone their ways to the towns. But my hubby and me, we reared our children here among the sheep, and we want nothing different."

"Does the stream ever dry up?" asked Francis.

She shook her head.

"Not quite. The water comes from deep down. Even in the drought year, when all the fields were yellow, there was always a trickle, and our pasture stayed green. Now we must be going, son, or we'll miss the mail truck."

Francis said a rather sad good-bye to the source, the pet lamb, and the buns, and he and the shepherd's wife went down the other side of the hill together. It was only a little way to the main road and the mailbox, and Francis was surprised to see the long shadows and the bright evening sky. It seemed such a short time since morning.

"Look in again, dearie, if you're ever along this way," said the shepherd's wife, as he jumped into the obliging postman's truck. "It's been a pleasure. You'll be home in no time."

It was certainly much quicker by the main road, and the mailman went right through Upper Bowbridge and dropped him at the garage. He picked up his bicycle and pedaled home. The sun was setting when he arrived, and the family was in a high state of alarm. In fact, Uncle John was out looking for him. Unfortunately, Kate saw him first.

"You deserve to be shot, Francis," she burst out, "frightening Mum and Dad and wasting their time like that! I wasn't frightened in the least. I knew you'd gone off just to get out of helping, you lazy little horror!"

"Just a minute, Kate." Aunt Alison appeared with Martin and Chris, wide-eyed behind her. "Where have you been, Francis? It was very naughty indeed of you to run away like that. We've all been very anxious about you."

Francis gazed at her. He had had a wonderful day, but he was not going to talk about it in front of Kate—he had not done anything naughty. Later on, when they had all stopped being cross, he would tell Auntie Alison about the source.

And she, seeing that far-away look of glory in his eyes, decided to let her husband tell him that he was to stay at home next day and do his share of work instead of going to the cattle market. She would find out where he had been first. He certainly did not look as though he had been back with his gang, slashing tires.

Tea was over, but she had kept him some, and she sat by him as he ate. Uncle John had returned, greatly relieved to find Francis home, and had gone off to the calves.

"Where have you been all day, Francis?" she said severely. "You must tell me."

Francis turned a radiant face toward her. "I found the source," he said simply. "Not the source of the big river—that's far away in big mountains, I think—it might take you days and days to walk there—but there was a little stream—and the grass was so green—and I followed it right to the top of the hill, and I found the source, Auntie. I really did. It came up out of the earth, clear like glass, and I put my feet in it, and the shepherd was angry 'cause you must never foul sources, Auntie. Sheep won't drink fouled water. And then he wasn't angry anymore, and he took me into his house, and there was a little tame lamb—and she gave me cups of tea and buns—I ate six—"

"Who did, Francis?"

"The shepherd's wife. She feeds the pet lamb. His

father found the spring, and it was deep underground
but the grass was green—and he cleared away all the
mud and muck and dead leaves, and the water bubbled up clean, and they've lived there ever since—
and it never dries up, not even in drought, and the
grass is always green. And I came home in the mail
truck. Oh, and the garage man gave me a bag of
chips, and I saw a kingfisher and lots of rabbits—
and, oh! I forgot! I picked you some forget-me-nots.
They are in my bike basket, and I think they might be
dead."

She smiled and rumpled his hair.

"You've had a wonderful day, Francis," she said,
"but next time you must ask. Your eyes are half shut.
You're nearly asleep. Run up to bed."

12

The Tulip Bed

But Francis did not get off quite as lightly as he had hoped, because directly after breakfast Uncle John called him aside and explained to him that his share of work was still waiting to be done and that he would have to stay and do it instead of going to the cattle market. "I'm sorry," said Uncle John, "but there will be other cattle markets, and we are all disappointed. We would have enjoyed it much more with you, but you've got to learn some day, haven't you!"

Francis was bitterly disappointed, but much too proud to show it, so he shrugged his shoulders and wandered off with his nose in the air. There was one small gleam of comfort. Kate would not get her quiet day now, for he would see to it that there was as much noise as possible.

Uncle John showed him exactly what he had to do, and then there was a general flurry of departure: sandwiches and thermoses being prepared for the market party and Auntie Alison bustling around the kitchen, straightening up.

"I'll see to all that, Mum," said Kate. "Do hurry, or you'll miss your bus."

"Right," said her mother, "but don't bother about lunch. We'll do something quick when I come in. Oh, and keep an eye on Francis and take him a snack."

Kate wrinkled up her nose and locked the living room so that the question of "Chopsticks" would not arise. Francis was a pest! Already his loud, tuneless singing came floating through the kitchen window, and surely his weeding need not involve all that banging about. She tidied the kitchen meticulously, shut the window, and carried her essay to the front of the house where she could be rid of him. She wished she need not take him a snack because he did not deserve it, so she prepared him some weak lemonade and two soft cookies halfway through the morning and marched out to the yard. To her astonishment and indignation, the work was hardly begun, and Francis was strolling up from the river.

Kate let fly at him. "You lazy lout," she exclaimed, "you've hardly begun! You'd bettter get cracking, 'cause there's no dinner for you until you've finished."

Francis sat down on a barrel and stared at her coldly.

"I shan't do it at all unless I want to," he said, "and I'm not doing what you say, anyhow, Big Boss. I'm not your slave, and I shall do what I like. I shan't stay here at all unless I want to."

Kate lost her temper. Her face flushed crimson, and all she had longed to say for the past month came pouring out in a torrent. "I wish you wouldn't," she shouted. "Nobody wanted you in the first place. You just invited yourself, and Mum and Dad were kind enough to take you in, and you never lift a finger to help them! You're ungrateful, Francis, and you're cruel too. We know all about your throwing stones at the ducks, and you're a liar too—all those silly stories you told the boys about guns and bombs!

Even Chris knew they weren't true. It's all a pack of
lies, and you are just a show-off, and we wish you'd
go back to where you came from!"

She turned and ran. Francis picked up the mug of
lemonade and flung it after her. It just missed her
head and broke into bits on the wall. Then he stood
very still, breathing hard, his eyes smoldering in his
white face. Only one remark of Kate's had stuck in
his mind. *"We wish you'd go—nobody wanted you in
the first place!"*

Was it true? They had all seemed so pleased to
see him, and he had felt so sure of himself and so safe.
If it was true, then he was leaving, right now, that
very minute. But he had to vent his hatred and misery
on something or someone first. It was no good attack-
ing Kate; she was too big. So he looked around and
found himself staring at the sun-warmed colors of the
yard—wallflowers, polyanthus under the lilac, and
Auntie Alison's prize tulip bed in full flower.

He went to the weeping willow, broke off a switch,
and walked over to the tulips. Standing in front of
them, he deliberately switched the head off every stem.
Backwards and forwards he went with a fierce,, miserable sort of enjoyment. It took quite a time, and when
he had finished there was not a flower left standing.

Kate stormed her way back to the kitchen and then
sat staring out the window. Now that her temper was
cooling off she was beginning to feel deeply ashamed
of herself. *How could I have said that?* she thought.
*I was worse than him! And besides, it's not true—
Mum and Dad did want him. They'd hate it if he went
away.* She sat thinking for a while and then got up
and walked very slowly back to the yard. Perhaps she
could tell him that that bit had been a mistake, and

they had wanted him even though he was such an awfully lazy, cheeky little liar. But he was not where she had left him. He was standing by the tulip bed, and she saw him fell the last beautiful, crimson head to the ground.

She rushed at him, but he saw her coming and shot out of the garden gate and dodged behind the house. She did not follow him; it was too late. She knelt beside the ruined tulip bed, trying desperately to lift a few of the bruised stems and leaves, but nothing could be done.

"And Mum loved them so much," mourned Kate. "She planted them all herself and was going to pick them for the church. Whatever shall I say to her?"

She was conscious of the rattle of a bicycle bouncing over the cobblestones. "Francis," she shouted, "come here!" But he hurled back a rude remark and was gone, so she went into the house and sat down in front of her schoolbooks and wept with frustration and worry. How much of his reaction had been her fault? And what was Mum going to say when she told her all about it?

Her mother came gaily into the kitchen about one o'clock. "Kate," she called, "where are you? Come and tell me if you like my new hairstyle. And what a treat the kitchen looks! You *are* a good girl!"

Kate came in, and her mother turned, surprised at her silence. The girl stood there crimson-cheeked, and she looked as though she had been crying.

"Kate," cried her mother, "has something happened?"

"Yes, Mum. Francis has gone, and you'd better come and look at the tulip bed."

They went out and stood looking at the ruin. Mrs.

Glenny gave a little sigh. "Well, that's that!" she said sadly. "I'm glad that at least we saw them come out. But whatever happened? He must have gone berserk to do a thing like that! And where's he gone?"

"I don't know, Mum. He was so lazy and wouldn't work—and—well, I said things to him and some of them were true—but some of them weren't. I really lost my temper, Mum. He was so cheeky!"

"Let's eat," said her mother gently, "and you can tell me then. He'll come back before dark like he did yesterday. I'll fry some bacon and eggs, and you make some tea."

When they were sitting in front of a hot meal, Kate tried to tell her story, and her mother listened rather gravely. Kate was so dutiful and hard working, but her impatient attitude toward Francis had worried her mother all along. "I told him he was lazy, Mum, and that's true," said Kate, "and I told him we knew about him throwing stones at the ducks, and the cows sometimes, and I said he was a liar. That's true, too—all those stories he told to Martin and Chris!"

"The bombs and guns weren't true," said her mother, "but it probably wasn't all lies. He really has been involved with a very rough gang, and that's what worries me when he disappears. Was that all you said to him?"

"No," said Kate softly, looking at her plate. "I said he'd invited himself, and we'd never wanted him—and I said we wished he'd go away."

"Oh, Kate, what a thing to say! No wonder he wanted to destroy something! Besides, it isn't true. I wanted him from the moment he rushed in from the river looking like a drowned rat. There was something about him—I was thrilled when he came back.

How could you say a thing like that?"

"But, Mum," pleaded Kate, "he ought to be punished! You and Dad are too lenient with him. You'd never let Martin be lazy and steal food and tell lies like he does. It isn't fair!"

"We do tell him, and Dad punished him this morning, but do you know his story? He told us himself, and his Granny has written twice about it, so we know it is true. Martin has known nothing but love all his life, and he's never had anything to hate. Francis's father left him when he was a baby, and the second husband has never wanted him. Now the stepfather has gone off with another woman, and the divorce is on the way, and his mother is in a psychiatric hospital. It's been jealousy, quarreling, and hating for years on end.

"Francis needs healing before scolding. We have to go a step at a time. As soon as he feels quite sure that he is loved and wanted just like our own children, then we can start dealing with the other things. And he was just beginning to get there. Something happened to him yesterday. I don't quite know what, but finding that spring was really meaningful to him."

"And now I suppose I've spoiled it all! Oh, Mum, I'm sorry!"

"Well, there'll be another chance, I'm sure. The thing is to discover where he is. I wonder if he could have gone back to that shepherd's wife. I've no idea where he found her."

"He cycled over the bridge, not along the river road. Could he have gone back to his own house?"

"I shouldn't think so. There's no one there. He'd hardly go to an empty house. We'll wait till Dad comes home with the car. Francis may easily come back alone. After all, he's had no dinner, and he likes his food."

But Kate was less hopeful. After lunch she wandered sadly out into the yard and stood watching a hedge sparrow dart to and fro and then settle on her bright eggs. *Hedge sparrows' nests are so cozy,* thought Kate, and she looked back to the shabby farmhouse where they had all grown up, loved and secure. She had taken it all for granted. She had never quite realized before how rich she was, how much she had to give and share.

"Oh, God," she whispered, "please bring him back. It was partly my fault, and I want him here very much."

13

The River of Life

Francis cycled madly across the bridge and swerved into the village street. Had any fast car been coming, that would have been the end of him. But the road was almost empty except for a few children playing round the old forge under the chestnut tree, and nobody stopped him. Then the hill outside the village slowed him down, and, for the first time, he started to consider his position.

Where was he going?

He was never, never going back to the farm. That was certain. Nobody wanted him. "We wish you'd go back to where you came from." That was what Kate had said, and if it was true, then all he had trusted in was an awful mistake. Mums and dads were probably the same all the world over; they just wanted their own children, like his own stepfather. And Mum, to whom he belonged, was in a hospital, and perhaps she would die, and then there would be nobody. "Mum, Mum," he whimpered, and sat down between the roots of a large chestnut tree to think out the next step.

The great roots encircled him, and when he looked up into the foliage he noticed that the flowers stood up like lighted candles. *Like a Christmas tree,* he thought idly, and a great wave of homesickness swept over him. Last Christmas had been a happy time. They had all had presents, and no one had quarreled all day long. They had been too busy playing with their toys.

He suddenly longed for his toys and his other things—his dinky cars and stamps and football cards. And his set of magic tricks and his Lego. He had not missed them till now because there had been so much to do at the farm, indoors and out. But those delights were his no longer. He suddenly decided to go back to his own house and sit for awhile in his own room and play with his own toys. There might even be a can of something in the pantry, and when he got there he would make up his mind about what to do next. Perhaps when it began to get dark, Mrs. Glengarry would have some suggestions. She always took in stray cats, so why not stray boys?

He was not worried about getting in. Some time ago he had been locked out, and he had found a secret way in. You climbed onto the roof of the little front porch and scrambled up a drainpipe. There was a loose catch on his own bedroom casement window, and a child's small fingers could pry those windows far enough apart to reach inside and push up the catch. It had seemed such a convenient secret to possess that he had never told anyone, and no one had noticed.

He got up and pedaled steadily on, calmed and comforted by the peace of the April countryside. The hawthorn smelled sweet in the sunshine, and the banks were a riot of campions, bluebells, and garlic mustard. He seemed to be pedaling to the rhythm of birdsong. No one noticed him as he reached the suburb of the city and turned into his own road. A moment later, he slipped into his own yard and stood, half afraid, looking round.

It looked like a wild garden, for April had caught up with it. The grass had grown long, and the small flower bed that Mum had planted was choked with weeds. But the house inside would surely be the same, and he suddenly longed for Whiskers. He would have to get hold of Whiskers somehow, although she had become an excellent mouser and might not at all wish to leave the barn.

He wandered around the house and garage and noticed, to his surprise, that the kitchen window had been broken and boarded up with wood and nails. He wondered who had done that. Probably Wendy had done it with her ball after he left.

The kitchen reminded him of food, and he prowled round to the porch where he climbed up onto the windowsill and out onto the porch roof. The next part was harder and much more dangerous because the pipe might break, but it could be done. There were two joints on which to rest his feet, and then a pull across to the edge of the window, and you landed on his bedroom windowsill. Yes, he could still get his fingers through the crack, although they seemed to have gotten much fatter at the farm. A wriggle, and the catch lifted, and then he was letting himself down under the curtains, back into his own little bedroom. He pulled back the curtains joyfully and the light streamed in. Then he stood rooted to the spot, staring, and his heart gave a little lurch of fear.

Someone had completely vandalized his room. His drawers were overturned, his stamp album torn, his football cards ripped up, his soldiers scattered and mostly smashed. The wheels had been pried off many of his dinky cars, and his precious comics had been torn and trampled on. Whoever had been in had done the job very thoroughly indeed. Francis gave a little cry of grief and terror and shot down the stairs and out the front door. All he wanted to do was to get away from this terrible house as soon as possible.

Where could he go now? His toys had been his last real link with home, and now there was nowhere. But almost without knowing it, his feet had carried him across the yard to his refuge in the cherry tree. The blossoms were over now, but the leaves would hide him from view, and he could sit and cry as much as he wanted. He seized the bough and stopped again to recover from his second great shock.

A small pair of brown legs dangled from the bough above, and a cautious brown face peered down at him. "Francis," whispered Ram, "you come up and I tell you all."

Had Francis found Ram in his private tree at any other time, he might have been angry, but just at that point he was overjoyed. He clambered up, and Ram's huge black eyes scanned him anxiously and lovingly. When he realized that Francis was pleased to see him, he beamed.

"I saw your bike, Francis, and I saw you climb," said Ram shyly. His English had improved a lot in three weeks. "So I sit here till you come out. What have they done in your house?"

"Who?" asked Francis. "Who broke my toys and tore up my stamps and my cards? Everything is torn and broken and spoiled, Ram." His voice trembled, and he squeezed the bough above to keep from crying.

"Tyke and Spotty," said Ram. "When you went away they follow me every day from school. They ask and they ask where you gone. I said I don't know. And they said they go to beat you up because you tell the police about their little house."

"I never did," sniffed Francis.

"Then one day I come from school, and I saw them at your gate looking at your house. They point. They talk. I watch round the corner till they go away, and I tell my mother. Then I came and I climb the cherry tree, and I watch till it get dark, and the next day and the next day, and after two days they come."

"What did you do?"

"I watch very quiet. I saw them break the glass and open the window, and Tyke he go in and open the door, and they all go in. Then I drop into that other yard, and I runned and runned, and I phone 999 the police, and I tell them boys in your house."

Francis gazed at him in wide-eyed admiration. Here was true adventure! Ram was wonderful. A real hero!

"They come in three police cars," said Ram, waving his hands and talking very fast. "And they stop down the street. I watch and I watch round the corner. Then they came back with Tyke and Spotty, and they all went away in the cars."

"But what happened? Where are they now?"

"I haven't seen them anymore, but the boys say they will not come back to our school. They go to another school where they stay all day and all night, and they never go home. And when I came back here someone had put wood in the window, and now no one more can come into your house. I came every day, Francis, and I climb the cherry tree to see that all is good with your house."

They sat talking for a long time, all about Tyke and the broken toys and the fire. It was nearly tea-time when Francis remembered that he had had no dinner. He suddenly decided to go home with Ram, have something to eat, and stay the night. Perhaps Mrs. Ram would adopt him till Mum came home.

He explained the situation to Ram, who was not quite sure about his father's reaction. There was no spare bed, and his own was very narrow, but perhaps he could give Francis that bed and sleep on the couch. They climbed down and started home, but just as they reached the gate a car drew up. Auntie Alison jumped out, and not even Francis could mistake the relief on her face, although she greeted him in quite a matter of fact way. "Come along, Francis," she said. "It's time to come home, and you must be so hungry. Is this Ram? We've heard about you, Ram."

Francis scowled at her.

"I'm not coming," he whispered. "You don't want me. You never did want me. Kate said so. I'm going to live with Ram."

"But it's not true. Kate lost her temper, and she knew it wasn't true as soon as she'd said it. We all want you. We've been looking for you all day and longing for you to come home. Nobody wanted any supper till you were found. Won't you believe me, Francis?"

The word "supper" probably did the trick, and anyhow he knew that Auntie Alison always spoke the truth. Besides, he suddenly found that the farm was the one place where he wanted to be. "All right," he said drearily, "but they broke all my toys. All my stamps and my football cards, they're all torn up on the floor. Tyke did it. Ram saw him."

"And my tulips are all broken and lying on the ground," said Auntie Alison. "Francis did it, and Kate saw him. But we still want you."

Francis hung his head. "Sorry," he muttered. He had almost forgotten about the tulips.

"It's all right. We'll talk about it later, and we've forgiven you. Will you come home now?"

He slipped his hand into hers. "Come and see my toys," he said. "Tyke did it, and Ram saw him and told the police. Ram, when I come home, we'll play every day. And Auntie, could he come and play at the farm?"

"Of course. Any Saturday. Uncle John could pick him up sometimes with the cattle feed." She smiled down into Ram's eager brown face, and Ram ran home in ecstasy, his faithful heart bursting with pride and joy.

"You'll have to wait at the door," said Francis, and she watched, her heart in her mouth, till his legs disappeared through the bedroom window. *The child's a born burglar,* she thought to herself, and then he reappeared at the door and led her upstairs. He pulled her down beside him on the rug amid the wreckage.

"All my toys!" he mourned, "and my comics and my stamps. All spoiled!" And his tears flowed afresh.

She put her arm around him and tried to comfort him. "Not all spoiled," she said. "Lots of the stamps aren't torn, and if you soaked them off in water, you could stick some of them in a new album. And look! There's a dinky truck under the bed, not broken."

They salvaged what they could, and he leaned against her, worn out and wretched. He had never before seemed so near to her, but how could she make him understand?

"You know now what it feels like, don't you," she said gently, "when people smash and destroy and hurt. I wonder why Tyke did this, and I wonder why you broke all those tulips? It didn't make anyone happy did it?"

He thought about it, sniffing sadly.

"I suppose it's something bad inside us," he said at last. "But Tyke's bad all the time, and I'm not always bad. I wasn't bad yesterday."

The word "yesterday" gave her an idea.

"I think our hearts inside us are rather like that spring you found," she said. "It was fouled at the source, full of dirt and dead leaves and the water was all muddy."

He looked up, alert and interested.

"The sheep wouldn't drink it," he said. "They'll never drink water what's fouled at the source."

"No, I don't blame them. But Francis, I know where hurting and smashing and destroying come from. They come from hearts that are all fouled with hate and selfishness and unkindness, and then streams of hate and selfishness and unkindness flow out, like they did here. And then everyone is miserable."

He was listening quietly, so she went on.

"The shepherd had to clear away all the mud and dead leaves and make a fresh outlet for the spring. And what happened then?"

"The water came out all clear and ran to the river, and the grass was all green."

"Yes. And I'll tell you something Jesus said about

the source of a river. You can learn it by heart at home. Jesus said, 'If any man is thirsty, let him come to Me and drink. He who believes in Me, as the Scripture said, "From his innermost being shall flow rivers of living water." But this He spoke of the Spirit, whom those who believed in Him were to receive.' "*

"A river of life," said Francis suddenly.

"Yes. Where did you hear that?"

"I dreamed it. And I think they once said it in church."

"Well, it just means this, Francis. When we feel sorry about our fouled source of hate and unkindness, we can ask Jesus to forgive it all and to take it away. Then we can ask Him to put His loving Holy Spirit into our hearts—and then there's a new spring, and clean streams of love and happiness and kindness flow out from Him, and then you become a loving, happy boy."

Francis was thinking. If they were all coming home to this smashed-up house, they would need a bit of love and happiness. Could it ever be different? Perhaps it could, if he was different.

"Would I really?" he asked.

"Yes. Not all at once, but little by little. Shall we ask Him?"

So they prayed together, there on the floor, amid all the wreckage of hate and unkindness. Auntie Alison prayed aloud that God would forgive all the anger, that Jesus would come right into Francis's heart, and that His Holy Spirit would be a new, clean source from which rivers of love and happiness would flow. Francis asked too, quietly in his heart.

He felt healed and peaceful as they drove home,

*John 7:37-38.

and no one welcomed him more wholeheartedly than Kate. But his real moment came later, sitting on the rug at prayer time, when he happened to look up and found himself staring at the card on the wall.

And suddenly he knew. He had found the answer to that first question he had asked over three weeks ago, "Where is God?" For if God came to us in Jesus, and if Jesus had come into his heart, then he had found God. God was right there within him, the source of a beautiful, clean river; for God was love.

14

The Swan

It was a very great relief to Francis, when he went back to school, to be rid of Tyke and Spotty. Their shadows no longer haunted the playground, and his teacher found him quite changed. A month's freedom from fear and anxiety had made a big difference in him. He had put on weight and was alert and attentive in class. In short, he was happy.

And night by night he was learning more of those wonderful stories of Jesus, whom he knew had come to live in his heart, although he had not yet discovered what difference that made. He knew he was happier, but then there were other reasons for that. Mum was getting better, Tyke was out of the way, and Kate had become quite friendly and motherly. And over and above all, there was the river.

His love for the river grew as the days lengthened into summer, and he would wander off after tea, sometimes with Martin, sometimes alone, to launch the little boat or to wade over to the reed islands. On Saturdays Ram would join them, and they would run along to their special swimming place and swim lazily with the current and then scramble out and run back along the bank and dive in again. Martin and Chris, who had lived all their lives by the river, sometimes

wondered what Francis found so exciting and would
go off and do something else, but Francis spent nearly
all his spare time, in, on, or by the river.

He woke one morning because the sun was shining
right through the open window onto his face. It had
just appeared over the rising wheat fields, and Francis
knew that it must be very early, too early to wake
Martin. He stuck his head far out and looked around.
Even the cows were not stirring, yet every bird in
Warwickshire seemed to be fluting, twittering, or car-
oling in the apple trees. He thought that if he went
very quietly into the yard, he might see them all sitting
in rows. He slipped on his clothes and his sandals and
let himself out the front door.

He could not see the birds, and yet they were all
around him in the lilac and the apple boughs. The
yard lay in shadow, and the grass was cold and heavy
with dew and cobwebs. The mists still lay on the river,
tangled in the alders and weeping willows. Everything looked strange and mysterious, and Francis
walked very softly, almost as though he were afraid
to disturb the unawakened world.

He ran along the bank as fast as she could because
he wanted to go a long way. No one would mind his
being late for breakfast on a Saturday, but he must
not be too late because Ram was coming. The sun
soon caught up with him, stealing down across the
fields, turning the dew to silver, setting the buttercups
alight and scattering the mists. The shadows of the
trees still lay across the river, and he thought he could
run for a long, long way, past where the streams met,
and not turn back till he reached the bridge in the next
village. He had never been farther downstream than
that before.

But the morning was so bracing and the sunshine
so golden, that he seemed to reach the bridge in no
time, running all the way because he felt so strong
and light, and the church clock, rising above the yew
trees, only pointed to seven o'clock. He would run
on, on, and on, farther than he had even been before,
and find out where the river went next.

The countryside seemed wilder beyond the bridge,
and the river was mostly hidden by thick hazel bushes.
Woods came down almost to the banks—deep woods
where the ferns had sprung up above the dying bluebells and cuckoos called incessantly. He was thinking
of turning back when suddenly the banks receded, the
river broadened, and he found himself in a reedy,
shallow place with little gravel beaches and marshy
backwaters where rushes grew. It was an interesting
place where gnats danced on the surface of the water
and the first swallows skimmed the pools. He sat
down under a weeping willow, for the morning was
already hot, and looked about him.

And then he saw her coming—a magnificent white
swan, turning her head from left to right, and Francis
cowed behind the tree, for he knew that swans can be
very fierce. She did not seem to see him, but she
scented danger and made a strange hissing sound.
Then she floated to the edge of the current in among
the reeds, walked across the beach, and into the backwater.

Francis crept from his hiding place, lay flat on the
grass, and peeped over the edge of the bank. There
was a nest, roughly built in a hollow in the rushes, and
on the nest lay four green-white eggs.

Francis was thrilled. He had found it, he alone—
the nest that Martin had so often talked about. He

wanted one of those eggs more than anything else in
the world at that moment, and no one need ever know.
They would think it a terrible crime at the farm to take
a swan's egg, but he need not tell them. He could
hide it under his clothes in his drawer, and on Monday
he would take it to school and show his friends. It was
a wonderful, rare thing to find a swan's nest, but unless he took an egg, who would ever believe him?

Of course, he would have to wait till the swan
moved. She was now sitting firmly on her nest, but if
he could alarm her a little or disturb the water, she
might go away. He forgot all about breakfast and the
time. He even forgot about Ram. He thought he
could wait forever if only he could hold that warm,
smooth egg in his hands.

He waited so long and lay so still that he almost
fell asleep to the chatter of the shallow river. Suddenly he was jerked awake, for the swan had risen
and stretched out her gleaming wings. She pushed
through the reeds and launched herself on the stream.
Just a little wriggle now, and he could seize that egg.

But while he was actually stretching out his hand,
something happened. He knew it was wrong, and he
suddenly did not want to do it. And that was a
strange feeling, for he had never minded doing wrong
before, if it was something he wanted to do badly. It
was such a queer feeling that he drew back his hand
and lay looking at the swan and thinking how beautiful she was. Suddenly he discovered that he cared
about that swan, and he did not want her to come back
and find her egg gone. And that was queer too, because he had never much minded hurting animals before. He wanted to come back himself and share her
joy, and watch the eggs hatch into nestlings, and show

them to Martin and Chris and Ram.

He got up and started running in the direction of home, knowing that he was different and wondering what had happened to him. *It must be something to do with Jesus in my heart,* he thought. *I suppose that's how He talks to me. I suppose, if I listen, He'll always make me mind doing bad things.* And he knew that somehow those clear streams of love and happiness had started to flow.

He thought he had never felt so happy before, nor run so fast. Wet and dirty, he burst in on the family members, who were still sitting at their late Saturday breakfast. "I've found a swan's nest with four eggs!" he shouted. "Who wants to come and see it?"

Everyone wanted to see it, so they took a picnic lunch to the place, Mum and Dad bringing the food in the car, and the children walking. It was a glorious sun-drenched day, and Francis's happiness overflowed as he led them, one by one, to the backwater in the reeds. And late that evening, when Ram had gone home, Auntie Alison found him sitting quietly on the step, stroking Whiskers.

"You're getting like your namesake," she said, sitting down beside him. "You and your nests and your cat!"

"Who's my namesake?" asked Francis.

"Don't you know? It's a beautiful name. Francis of Assisi lived about seven hundred years ago in Italy. He loved birds and other wild creatures so much that he used to go out into the fields and preach to them. They say that they all used to come close to him and listen."

"I don't believe it. How could birds listen?"

"I don't expect they did, but it looked like it, and

the people in those days believed it. I expect his heart was so full of the love of God that it just flowed out and everybody felt it, even the birds and the animals."

"Like you said—like rivers flowing out. Will you show me that book tomorrow?"

"Yes, I'll find the parts you'd understand. Now, come in. It's bedtime."

But he lingered a little longer with his cheek resting on Whisker's fur, listening to the song of the river. The same gurgling water that he could hear washing the roots of the alders would flow down under the bridge to the backwater where the swan sat with folded wings. How glad he felt that she was sitting on four warm eggs.

15

The Homecoming

It was mid-June when Granny came to visit Francis. Uncle John met her on the bus in the village and drove her to the farm because she was rather lame and walked with a stick. She was sitting in the living room when Francis raced in from school on Wednesday afternoon.

He was glad to see his grandmother because there were many things he wanted to ask her, and he always felt safe and comfortable with her. They had tea by themselves, and Francis bombarded her with questions, and the answers were most satisfactory. Mum was better and coming home Monday evening. She wanted to get there first and arrange things. Granny was going up to Yorkshire to get the little girls and bring them home by train on Tuesday evening. Because there was no school on Tuesday, Francis could go over and join his mother that morning. Granny was going to stay with them for a time and help.

"Why do you have to go?" asked Francis. "Why doesn't Dad bring them home in the car? And when's he coming, anyhow?"

Granny cleared her throat. "Francis," she said at last, "I have to tell you something very sad."

"What?"

"Your father's not coming back. He's going to marry somebody else."

"Oh, yes. Gloria!" said Francis calmly. "I wondered if it would come to that. Poor old Mum!"

Granny looked both shocked and startled.

"I had no idea you knew anything about it, Francis," she said. "It's a terrible thing for your mother. And how do you think Wendy and Deborah will take it?"

"I 'spect they'll be sad," said Francis thoughtfully. "After all, he was their own dad. But I'll look after them all, Granny. I'm ten now. We'll have to get the house cleaned up, won't we? You heard how Tyke messed up my room, didn't you? But Auntie Alison and I went and took care of that."

She smiled at his eager, important voice. *Perhaps things will be easier for him now,* she thought. *There'll be room for him and a real place. What a splendid boy he is!*

"I know," she replied. "I've been in. Mrs. Glengarry's going to dust around, and get in some food, and air the beds, so it won't be like coming to an empty house. But the yard's terrible! Do you think Mrs. Glenny would let you go over on Saturday and do a bit of weeding and watering? It's been such a hot week, and all the plants are dying."

Francis nodded. That would be fun. He would attach the hose to the kitchen tap and make little rivers all over the flower bed, and everywhere the rivers came, Mum's plants would grow green. He just could not wait.

Uncle John was working on the baler. The grass and moondaisies and ragged robin were almost knee-deep in the meadow, and it was time to start the haymaking. Francis went and stood beside him.

"Uncle John," he said. "When you go in to town on Saturday morning, could you drop me and my bike off at home? I want to get the yard ready for Mum, and I'll come back when it is finished."

"Good idea," said Uncle John, "and perhaps the others could go for an hour and help too. And when I pick them up, I'll cut the grass. It must be like a jungle now. You can stay behind and come when you're ready. There's that nice old cat-lady next door, isn't there, if you want anything?"

Francis trotted off, delighted, to find Auntie Alison, who was peeling potatoes. "Well, Francis," she said. "I hear you're leaving us. We shall miss you."

"I shall come back lots," he said. "I shall come on Saturdays to see the river—and you and Uncle John and Kate and Martin and Chris. And I shall come on Sunday to church, and sometimes I shall bring Ram— and Auntie, Mum's coming on the bus, and it stops at the bottom of our road at six, and she thinks we're coming on Tuesday. Auntie, do you think I could give her a big surprise and get there first? She'd open the door and think the house was empty, and there I'd be—me and Whiskers. Wouldn't that be a lovely surprise?"

"Yes, I think it would," said Auntie Alison, laughing. "We'll keep it a dead secret. I'll take you over with your things about five o'clock and leave you there. And if by any chance she misses the bus or doesn't come, just phone us and we'll bring you back."

Saturday was a huge success. Uncle John mowed the lawn, and everybody weeded. It was only a small yard and Francis, fastening the hose to the tap in the kitchen, watered every dry, thirsty plant. *I think it will be all green by Monday,* he thought. *Wherever the water comes, it will be green.*

He got more and more excited as the weekend passed, and on Sunday evening Auntie Alison came up to say good night. "You'll have to be like the father of the family now, Francis," she said. "Your mother's going to need you so much. What a mercy she's got a boy of ten as well as those two little girls."

"Yes, I know. It's a funny thing, but I didn't really like my two sisters much before. Wendy pinched me, and Debby was such a crybaby, and Dad always said it was my fault. But do you know?—now I want to see them again."

"Yes, you'll have to look after them now. It's sad for them to lose their father, and I think you'll soon learn to love them. It has made a difference having Jesus in your heart, hasn't it? Do you remember your special Bible verse?"

"Yes, I think so. 'If any man is thirsty, let him come to Me and drink. He who believes in me,' as the Scripture said, 'From his innermost being shall flow rivers of living water'—something about the Spirit."

"Yes, the source is Jesus coming to you, and the rivers are His love flowing out of you, teaching you to love. And if He's in your heart, He'll be in your home too, and it will make all the difference. I am going to teach you one more thing that Jesus said, and we will underline both these verses in your Bible. Listen to this—"

She picked up the Bible that Uncle John had given him on Easter Sunday and found John, chapter 14.

"Jesus said, 'If anyone loves me, he will keep My word; and My Father will love him, and We will come to him, and make Our abode* with him.' You see, first He lives in the heart that loves and obeys Him, and then the rivers of love flow out into the home, and everything is different."

"I know." He spoke slowly, groping for words. "But when I get home—you see, it's not like here—we don't read the Bible at home—I mean, how shall I go on learning about Jesus?"

"I'll give you a little book that tells you what to read each day. Make a time every day to read it carefully, and pray about what you read. I know it is difficult alone. What about your Granny? Perhaps she could read it with you, and then perhaps Wendy would start listening too. I think she could understand."

"It would be a very good thing if Wendy learned about Jesus," said Francis seriously. "She might stop pinching."

"Yes, she might," agreed Auntie Alison, "but you'll have to be patient. It takes time."

She kissed him and left him. It was still light, and he could hear the rustle of wind in the ripening corn-field. *I'll pick a big bunch of poppies,* he thought, and wondered what the plants in the yard at home were looking like. *Everything grows green where the streams come,* he thought drowsily. *I'll have to pack tomorrow, and Auntie might let me make some flap-jacks like she did when Ram came.* He fell asleep thinking what fun it would be to sit, just he and Mum, at the kitchen table with a pot of tea and a plate of flapjacks.

At last it was four o'clock on Monday and time to go. He had been so excited about going home that he hardly realized, till he came to say goodbye, how

*Home.

sorry he was to leave the family, the cows, and the river. Whiskers was not at all pleased to leave the barn—there was not a hope of a mouse at 23 Graham Avenue!

"I'll come back soon," he called through the car window. " 'Bye everybody, and thanks for having me." He tried to wave, but it was difficult, for with one arm he was clasping Whiskers around her middle and with the other he clasped a huge summer bouquet of poppies, wild roses, ragged robin, and moondaisies. There would just be time to arrange them and get tea ready before Mum arrived.

They picked up the key from Mrs. Glengarry, and Auntie Alison helped him carry up his things to his room. Then she said good-bye, and he flung his arms around her middle and clung to her for a moment, realizing how happy he had been. Could it, would it last?

He arranged his flowers in bowls and pots all over the house, laid the tea things on the best cloth, and got out the best china cups and plates, for he believed this was what the occasion and his flapjacks deserved. Then he put on the kettle, very low, and went and curled up on the sofa by the living room window to watch the gate. He was not going to meet her at the bus stop; he was going to be her big surprise.

He began to wonder how he would welcome her. He wanted to appear very grown-up and capable, and he thought he would walk to the front door when he saw her coming, open it, and take her bag. "Don't worry, Mum," he would say. "I'm here, and I'll look after you and the girls, and tea's ready." He imagined himself looking very tall, almost a man, and Mum would say, "I'm so thankful you're here, Francis. I don't know what I'd have done without you, and whoever made these flapjacks?"

It was a lovely peaceful dream. Whiskers jumped onto his lap, and he threw his arm over the back of the sofa and rested his head on his hand. He gazed at the yard, where everything was green and flowering and pushing toward the sun. *It was my hose that did it,* he thought. *"Rivers of living water."*

He began to think about what Auntie Alison had said on Saturday night—*"Streams of love and happiness."* Well, he had been happy, and he had started to love others in a new way, others like Kate and the swan and the birds and the water rats and Ram and even Wendy and Debby. He was longing to see them again. Jesus said, "I will make my home with you"— if Jesus was there, perhaps they would all start again and be happy.

The time seemed very long. He was thinking so hard and feeling so tired after all the excitement that he half fell asleep, lulled by Whisker's purring. When at last his mother arrived, he never saw her come up the path nor did he hear the click of the key in the lock.

Francis's mother sat in the bus, her hands clasped tightly together. She was better and ready to start life again, but she almost regretted saying that she wanted to arrive first. The thought of the empty house frightened her now, and she did not want to be alone. There were too many sad things to remember, too many fears for the future. When the children came, it would be different. Or would it? Wendy and Debby would probably settle down. They were too little to understand much, and Granny was coming to live with them

for the present. But what had she done to her son,
Francis?

The thought of him had haunted her all through
her illness, and during her convalescence she would
wake in the night and remember those torn-up pictures in the rubbish bin, or the light that would die in
his eyes when he wanted to tell her something and she
just could not concentrate. All her thoughts had been
taken up with her anger and fear over her husband,
and she just had not had time for Francis. That was
why he had slipped away, got into bad company, and
ended up with strangers. Delinquent, her husband
had called him, and by whose fault?

She had heard from Granny that the strangers were
excellent people and that Francis was happy, and certainly his funny little letters all about calves, swans,
and streams sounded happy. But would she ever really
get him back, and would he ever forgive her? They
had thought at the hospital that she was grieving over
her husband, but they were wrong. That grief was
past, and she could only think of him with an angry
bitterness. Her grief was all for her son, now. It was
Francis, Francis all the time.

She walked slowly, for her bag was quite heavy,
and when she got inside the gate, she stopped to find
her key. She was surprised to see the yard looking so
good and the grass mowed. *It's that good old Mrs.
Glengarry next door,* she said to herself. *I'll pop over
when I've had a cup of tea.*

She crept into the house, awed by the tidy silence,
longing for her children. She would leave her bag in
the living room and put on the kettle. She went in and
then stood, rooted to the spot, wondering if she was
seeing things.

He lay curled upon the couch with Whiskers in his lap, his arm thrown over the back, his cheek resting on his hand. His eyes were almost shut, and as he suddenly looked up he seemed, for a moment, quite as bewildered as she was.

"Mum," cried Francis, and the next instant his arms were tightly around her neck. She held him close and knew, without another word being spoken, that her boy had come home.

Moody Press, a ministry of the Moody Bible Institute, is designed for education, evangelization, and edification. If we may assist you in knowing more about Christ and the Christian life, please write us without obligation: Moody Press, c/o MLM, Chicago, Illinois 60610.